PRICK

j. archer avary

First published in the USA by Leftover Books

ISBN 978992630701

'cactus family' original art by Emily Gustavson
cover design by J. Archer Avary

www.leftoverbooks.com

www.avary.co.uk

LEFTOVER
Books

(I WAS A) NEBRASKAN TEENAGE WEREWOLF

I was a Nebraskan teenage werewolf. I wore paisley rayon shirts and blue jeans with the cuffs rolled-up at the ankle. The year was 1990. I hung out with my friends Brad, Chad, and Circus Dan at Crossroads Mall.

Brad was a zombie, Chad was John Wayne Gacy, and Circus Dan was Frankenstein. We worked together in the haunted barn at Peabody's Pumpkin Patch. People from all over Omaha came to sip hot apple cider and have the living shit scared out of them. It was good clean fun.

The werewolf's primary responsibility was to wait at the end of a long, dark corridor, just around a sharp bend. A small TV showed the unsuspecting victims approaching. They never knew what hit them. Out jumped the werewolf and the people screamed with fear.

Every. Single. Time.

On paydays we hit the mall like a bunch of high rollers. Brad and Chad spent their entire paycheques on cassette tapes at Backspin Records. Circus Dan tried to impress girls from other schools by getting his ear pierced. It didn't work.

"You look like a dickhead with that thing," said Brad. "I hope it gets infected."

"He already looked like a dickhead," said Chad. "Now he looks like president of the dickhead society."

I thought the earring looked cool but didn't say so.

"At least I'm making an effort to meet girls from other schools," said Circus Dan. "We don't stand a chance with girls from our school because they know we're freaks."

I had my eye on a stylish pair of hiking boots. They looked entirely futuristic, made of blue-grey suede and accented with strips of fluorescent pink and blue leather. I had to have them but they were $75.

At the foodcourt Circus Dan ate like a king. He got the Lucky Panda combo plate with broccoli beef and sweet and sour pork. It came with pork fried rice, crab rangoon, and glow-in-the-dark dipping sauce. I bought myself a 99¢ egg roll.

"I don't eat chicken," said Circus Dan between bites. "My Mom says chicken is poor people's food."

"Poor people eat rice, dickhead," said Brad.

"My cousins are poor," said Chad. "The government gives them five pound blocks of cheese on the first of the month."

Brad and Chad sat there lamely, reading the lyric sheets of their respective purchases, watching us eat our

Lucky Panda. What did they know about poverty? They certainly weren't missing any meals. Still, I felt sorry for them and loaned them each a dollar so they could get an egg roll, on the condition they let me have their fortune cookies.

"Who eats those things?" said Brad. "They taste fucking stale."

"Only dickheads eat fortune cookies," said Chad.

I loved fortune cookies but didn't say so.

The biggest night at Peabody's haunted barn was Halloween. My voice was shot from weeks of howling like a werewolf. The crowds were steady, getting rowdier and more boisterous as the night wore on. Alcohol was involved, I could smell it strong on their collective breath.

A group of high school seniors came through the werewolf corridor and I scared the living shit out of them. The guy in front shrieked when I popped out, baring my sharp werewolf fangs. His friends laughed, and then the dickhead punched me in the face. I didn't see it coming.

I still had my black eye the next time we went to Crossroads Mall. I noticed girls from other schools looking at me and whispering to each other. The black eye was really working for me. I was a Nebraskan teenage werewolf in a paisley rayon shirt. I spiked my hair with gel and it hardened into a wall. I looked kind of dangerous. Maybe one of those girls would let me finger them someday.

I followed my friends to Backspin Records. The new Depeche Mode album was out. Brad and Chad each bought a copy.

"That makes no sense," said Circus Dan. "Just buy one and make copies. My dad's stereo has high-speed dubbing. That way we can all get a copy."

"Stuff it, turd," said Brad. "I need the actual cassette for my collection."

"I'm not letting you dickheads dub mine for free," said Chad. "I bought it with my own money. Get your own if you love Depeche Mode so much."

In 1990 it seemed like everyone loved Depeche Mode. I certainly did.

We took the escalator to the second level to the Athlete's Foot shoe shop. It was time to spend my haunted barn money. An employee dressed like a referee brought me a pair in my size and I tried them on.

"Turn them down," said Circus Dan. "They're burning my eyes."

"They make you look like a dickhead," said Brad.

"He already looked like a dickhead," said Chad. "Now he looks like a three-star general in the dickhead army."

"That's rich, coming from the king of all dickheads," I snapped. I couldn't let these boneheads disparage my fluorescent suede hiking boots. "These boots are cool. I'm going to wear them around school and start a new trend."

I scanned the foodcourt. Maybe we could get a table near some girls from other schools. We were pathetic in a way, teenagers already stuck in our habits. Circus Dan once again went for the Lucky Panda combo platter, and once again Brad and Chad were out of money. I had just enough leftover to buy an egg roll for each of us.

"See those girls," said Brad. "They're laughing at your boots."

I turned to look. Brad was right. Girls from other schools, laughing at me like I was some kind of loser. I bit through the crunchy fried exterior of my egg roll. I chewed and swallowed but tasted nothing.

"Can you believe he paid $75 for those?" laughed Chad. "What a dickhead."

Strangers pointed and laughed. I wanted to disappear but there was nowhere to hide. Was my attraction to these fluorescent suede hiking boots an attempt to assert my individuality or the sign of an undiagnosed personality defect?

I cracked open a fortune cookie and read it out loud. "It says a new pair of shoes would do you a world of good."

"The cookie is right," said Circus Dan. "You'll never get laid if you keep wearing those hideous boots."

WE THINK YOU'RE GOING TO LIKE IT HERE

I had a job lined up when I got to town, but the background check took ages. My start date was pushed back, which was fine with me. I'd rather explore my new city than suffer through a three-week insurance training course. I didn't want to seem aloof so I feigned major disappointment at the situation.

"What a bummer," I told the HR guy. "I was really looking forward to joining the team."

"We think you're going to like it here."

"Oh, I'm sure I will."

We hung up and I didn't think about the Hershey-Gurgler Insurance Company until my new start date.

Training was excruciating. I brought coloured pens and made elaborate sketches to keep myself awake. My training officer, Nigel, pulled me aside at the end of the day when all I wanted was to go the fuck home.

"I'm concerned with all the doodling during our training modules," said Nigel, peering over the wire-framed glasses perched on his nose. "Are my teaching methods failing to connect with your learning style?"

I didn't want to hurt his feelings.

"It's not that, exactly. The whole thing seemed very, um, interactive," I said, grasping for buzzwords. "I process information differently because my ADHD. I was diagnosed when I was four years old and haven't outgrown it yet."

That seemed to satisfy him. I was allowed to draw during class, as long as I put my pens and paper away when his boss came to observe the lesson. Nigel called it an accommodation, and sent everybody an email about the resolution, casting himself in a hero's light. He wanted to make a good impression on the higher-ups.

I passed my insurance underwriter's exam on the first try and graduated to the phones in the sprawling Hershey-Gurgler call centre. I was directed to a cluster of desks in the northwest corner. Everyone here sold the same product, Just Enough™ home insurance. The project manager shook my hand and introduced me to Ophelia. Her job was to help new recruits hone their skills on the phones.

"Just be yourself," she told me. "Most of our customers are so old they can barely comprehend their surroundings. They're so afraid of losing insurance coverage they'll take anything we offer."

It could've been easy but the process was bogged down with arcane corporate procedures.

Ophelia monitored our calls for quality assurance. The script was ten pages long. A lot could go wrong on the long and winding road from quote to closing. Ophelia critiqued our calls in breakout sessions with the Just Enough™ team. The vibe was casual. We leaned back in chairs and put our feet up on desks. I never paid attention to what was said until she talked about my calls.

"What you should've done when the call disconnected," she said, drawing out her vowels. "Was call back immediately to complete the quote. Since you didn't, it's classed as a QA fail."

It was easy to fail QA at Hershey-Gurgler. If you failed QA too many times in a given period they sent you back for additional training. Almost everybody got sent back for additional training.

"But they were on hold with me already because my computer crashed," I said, defensively. The last thing I needed was another three weeks in the training room with that boring-ass Nigel. "I told them to call back right away. Another Just Enough™ rep ran the quote and made the sale. Everybody's happy."

"You should've called them back right away. It's in the procedure manual."

I ticked the box to affirm I had read the procedure manual without actually reading it.

"Let me get this straight," I said. "I'm supposed to call this customer back right away, put them back on hold while I sit around with a thumb up my ass waiting for the guy from IT to fix my machine?"

"Your actions caused customer detriment, which according to procedures is a QA fail."

"Instead of being stuck on hold, the customer was able to renew their coverage. That seems like problem-solving to me."

"It's not your job to solve problems. You should've called them right back. Have you even read the procedure manual?"

"I think I skimmed it."

Ophelia moved on. The breakout session ended and we were back on the phones. It wasn't busy so I read a book while I waited for an incoming call.

There were a lot of rules about what you could and couldn't do between calls. The floor managers didn't like when you played Candy Crush on your phone or went to the bathroom, but it was perfectly acceptable to read a book at your desk. It was the only good part of the gig.

The project manager approached my desk with a somber look I recognised. "I need you to gather your things and come with me."

It grew silent in the Just Enough™ cluster. All eyes were on me as I packed my laptop, headset, and company-issued phone into a backpack. It was a long walk across the floor to the HR office where they sat me down. I chose to see the glass half-full. It wasn't even noon and I was about to get sent home to enjoy the rest of the day.

"This is a professional workplace and your, um, colourful language is not aligned with our corporate values," said the HR woman. "We received multiple complaints from team members that your behaviour has made them very uncomfortable."

"So what happens next?"

"Hershey-Gurgler is launching a gross misconduct investigation. When that's complete, management will invite you to a disciplinary hearing. Until then, you'll be placed on suspension with full pay."

I was escorted from the building. I took a last look around the call centre, basking in the sensations of this glorious moment. The sun was shining. Birds were singing in the trees. Rainbows streaked across the blue sky. It was almost like living a beautiful dream, only this was real. My greatest desire in life had always been to get paid to not work. At long last, it was happening.

I half expected Hershey-Gurgler to rush through the investigation to keep costs down, but the suspension dragged on for weeks, as if my salary was insignificant.

•

I didn't know what to expect at the hearing. The biggest section in the procedure manual was concerned with employee discipline. There were pages upon pages of potential outcomes. The hearing took place via telephone.

Was HR afraid I would become violent if I didn't like their decision?

"It's alleged you said, quote, 'I'll sit around with a thumb up my ass,' end-quote, during a breakout session," said the HR woman. She read the words robotically, without inflection.

"I admit using colourful language, but that doesn't rise to the level of gross misconduct," I said, thinking I had a strong case. I had seen enough Judge Judy to know the letter of the law was on my side. "Offensive language is listed as inappropriate behaviour in the discipline manual, and not gross misconduct. Dismissal for such a minor infraction would constitute a miscarriage of justice."

The HR department saw things differently. My paid suspension was over. I was officially terminated from the Hershey-Gurgler Insurance Company. At the end of the call they asked if I had anything to say for myself.

"I'm not the type to sit around with a thumb up my ass when I could get another job," I said. "I start at the post office next week."

SPECIAL DELIVERY

The mail was delivered by bicycle on the Island of Maricopa. As with most jobs, the new guy has to shovel the deepest shit, and that was no exception at the Maricopa Post Office. As its newest mail carrier, Frank Harper was learning this the hard way.

Shift Supervisor Roland Beckmann assigned him to the worst routes, the ones notorious for aggressive dogs and long steep driveways. Frank rolled his eyes when he saw his name next to Cliffside Portico, the worst route of them all.

"You're fucked, mate," said Barry Jenkins, who'd been with Maricopa Post for decades. "Forget about a lunch break. The rest of us will be out having pints after work and you'll still be on your route."

"Beckmann has it in for me. I got stuck on Cliffside Portico three times last week."

"That twat has it in for everybody. You're just the flavour of the month because you're new and from America."

"What route are you on?"

"High Street shuffle. Bloody piece of cake, that."

"Lucky bastard."

"Seniority has its advantages," grinned Jenkins. "Good luck, Frankie boy."

Frank gathered the day's mail and set off on his delivery bicycle, a single-gear beach cruiser. It had panniers and a massive basket bracketed to its handlebars to accommodate letters and parcels. Forget pedalling up the winding road to Cliffside Portico with a full load, it was easier to get off and push. By the time Frank reached the plateau, he needed a shit.

He clenched his cheeks together and carried on with his deliveries, pushing electric bills and other letters through the front door slots of Maricopa's most exclusive neighbourhood.

Cliffside Portico residents used their limitless disposable income to order random items from internet retailers. Some houses received three or four parcels a day. With panoramic sea views like these, Frank could understand why someone wouldn't want to leave their house to buy a titanium cheese grater.

It was none of Frank's business what these people were buying, but the shipping labels often gave it away. He learned early on that sex toy companies were particularly inept at the art of discretion.

"Good morning, ma'am," he said, extending his digital notepad to the occupant of a palatial estate. "Your shipment from the Erogenous Zone dot-com requires a signature."

His bowels cramped up as he walked back to his delivery bike. Whatever was brewing inside him was adamant to get out. Frank quickly delivered what mail was left on the cul-de-sac and pedalled post-haste to the Quick Brown Fox pub.

Frank leaned his bicycle against the granite wall and ducked inside. He handed the bartender a sheath of bills from beer distributors and made a beeline for the men's room. The single stall was wrapped in caution tape, with a small sign explaining that the facilities were out of order. Frank pushed open the stall door. There was a hole in the floor where a toilet should be, but no toilet.

"Fuck sake," muttered Frank.

He mulled his options. He could squat over the hole and empty his bowels into the hole like an animal, or he could carry on with his route and risk shitting himself.

He unbuckled his belt and began to pull down his trousers when two members of the construction crew walked in on him.

"Toilet's out-of-order, mate. You're gonna have to do your filthy business elsewhere," said the taller of the two men.

"But it's an emergency," Frank pleaded.

"Maybe so, but you can't just come in and defecate at our worksite," said the other guy. "It's a health and safety violation."

Frank fastened his belt and sighed. His need for relief was becoming urgent. The closest public toilet was at the far end of Cliffside Portico at the Thirsty Monk. With luck he could be pinching off a turd in about fifteen minutes.

He mounted his bike and pumped the pedals. This detour would put him an hour behind his already impossible schedule, but it was better than finishing the route in shit-caked trousers.

The urge to poo was overwhelming. Frank realised he wasn't going to make it to the Thirsty Monk and abandoned his bicycle. It was now or never.

He scaled a granite wall into a grassy field, pulled his trousers down around his ankles, and squatted, propping a hand against the wall to steady himself. He unclenched his cheeks and released a hot jet of diarrhoea into the tall grass. As Frank regained his breath, he noticed a woman watching him from the upstairs window of the house next door, covering her mouth in horrified disbelief.

The second wave came, then a third, until he was fully emptied out. He felt the woman's eyes on him as he pondered the logistics of cleaning up.

Just my luck, he thought. This old bird will be on the phone to report me to Beckmann faster than you can say special delivery.

Frank plucked a handful of grass and ambitiously attempted to wipe himself, a move that made more sense in theory than in practice. The blades of grass only succeeded at spreading the mess over a wider area. It was time for Plan B.

Frank wiggled out of his v-neck jumper and removed his undershirt. It was part of the official Maricopa Post uniform, but today it would be sacrificed in the name of basic hygiene. He wadded the shirt into a ball and cleaned himself, starting with his thighs before moving onto his undercarriage, then finally, his ring-piece and the thicket of coarse hair that surrounded it.

Frank tossed his soiled shirt towards the granite wall just as a strong gust came blowing in off the water, sending it airborne. The shirt sailed higher and higher, becoming lodged in the branches of a large elm tree where it flapped like a flag in the breeze, taunting him from above.

Frank fastened his trousers, pulled on his v-neck, and retreated to his bicycle. He had mail to deliver and was eager to get on with it. He took another look at the upstairs window where he'd seen the woman, but she had already disappeared. Probably grassing me up to Beckmann already, he thought.

By the time Frank finished his route, Maricopa Post Headquarters was deserted. He locked his bike in the shed and clocked out. When he returned to work the next day, Roland Beckmann was waiting for him.

"Let me explain how this works," he said. "Maricopa's Postmaster General is a very powerful man. He's determined that all the island's delivery routes, including Cliffside Portico, can reasonably be completed in fewer than seven hours. You can't expect to collect overtime pay when you fail to meet performance standards, can you?"

The Postmaster General must be a sadist, thought Frank. He shrugged. "I suppose not."

"Now that we're clear with the overtime policy, let's talk about the uniform policy."

"What about it?"

"I had a very interesting phone call from a member of the public yesterday, do you have any idea what that may have been about?"

Frank strained to keep his composure as he indicated the negatory.

"I took a phone call from a woman who said she witnessed one of our letter carriers riding around without a shirt under his v-neck jumper," said Beckmann. "Do you know anything about this?"

"Delivering mail without a shirt?"

"You fit the description. White male, average height, average build."

"That describes ninety percent of our workforce."

"Maybe so, but you were the only white male of average height and build working in Cliffside Portico yesterday."

"In this cold? I wouldn't be out there delivering mail without an undershirt. It doesn't make any sense."

Beckmann nibbled on his thumbnail. "That's what I thought. Maybe her eyes were playing tricks on her."

"Exactly," said Frank. "I know the importance of representing Maricopa Post in a professional manner when on the job. I take my appearance seriously."

Beckmann twisted his face into a robotic approximation of a smile.

"I know I can be a hard-ass at times, but I can tell you've had a tough week. I'm going to throw you a bone and put you on the High Street shuffle today. Don't screw it up, and don't get used to it."

They shook hands and Frank got the hell out of there. The last thing he needed was to be seen as one of Beckmann's lap dogs. As he sorted the day's mail, he felt a tap on his shoulder.

"Frankie boy," it was Barry Jenkins. "Moving up in the world, I see."

"I think Beckmann feels sorry for me. He said he was going to throw me a bone."

"That old chestnut," Barry sighed. "He's probably trying to set you up. Beckmann has stooges all over High Street. If anything goes wrong his little birdies will chirp it back to him."

"Thanks for the heads up."

An uneasy feeling brewed inside him as he pedalled towards the central business district. Not a shit, but something worse. Why would Beckmann feign kindness in one breath, then set him up with the next? Did he know more about yesterday's incident in the big grassy field than he was letting on?

Frank kept his head down and made his deliveries. Jenkins was right, the High Street shuffle was an absolute cakewalk. No hills, no dogs, and easy access to public toilets. The route was lined with shops and businesses where friendly proprietors offered him cups of coffee and sausage rolls. What a contrast to the hell-routes Beckmann usually threw at him.

By the time Frank sat down for lunch his mailbag was almost empty. He ordered liver and onions with black coffee and took out his phone.

He was greeted by an alarming number of Facebook notifications. He'd been tagged in a video post that was quickly going viral. It had amassed more than a thousand likes and hundreds of comments.

Frank clicked the link and was redirected to the Maricopa Mouthpiece, the island's unofficial home for sleazy gossip and unhinged political commentary. His jaw dropped when he saw the blustery headline, posted in a massive, all-caps font:

[EXCLUSIVE] MARICOPA POST EMPLOYEE DEFECATES IN ABANDONED FIELD

Frank scrolled through the poorly written article to an embedded video. The woman in the window had filmed everything, but instead of grassing him up to Beckmann, she sent the clip to the Maricopa Mouthpiece.

There he was, emptying his bowels for the whole internet to see. The video showed him in living colour, leaving no wiggle room for deniability. The waitress arrived with his liver and onions, but by then Frank had no appetite.

"Do you need any sauce?" she asked.

"I'll be okay," he said, more to himself than the waitress. This was a bad situation. When Beckmann saw the video, he'd be out on his ass looking for a new gig.

Frank noticed the waitress whispering to her coworkers behind the counter. She gestured in his direction and they struggled to suppress laughter. They must've seen the video in the Maricopa Mouthpiece.

He pushed away his plate, threw down a ten-spot, and bolted for the street. Bystanders pointed and laughed as Frank mounted his delivery bike. All of a sudden he'd become the most recognisable man on the Island of Maricopa.

He pumped the pedals as hard as he could. He had no direction, no destination, only a vague hope that his bicycle would carry him somewhere far far away.

CHAD THE INTERN

Geraldine got her wisdom teeth pulled. Her brother Chad wanted the codeine to sell at a house party in Council Bluffs. He picked her up from the dentist.

"Don't be such an unrealistic bitch," said Chad. "I can't give you half when I'm the one taking all the risk. These people carry knives."

"What about me?" she was groggy from the anaesthetic. "I don't think it's fair to suffer for anything less than fifty percent."

Chad stopped the car. "If you can't help me then I won't help you."

Geraldine didn't know what to say. Her brother was being a chode, as usual. "Are you kicking me out of your car?"

"I don't even know if I can sell this shit" said Chad. "I'm going to a party with Andrel. He's got acid for sale. I want to have some inventory just in case."

"Take the fucking codeine, then," said Geraldine. She produced a packet of pills from her purse and tossed it on the dashboard. "Have fun pretending to be a drug dealer."

"I'm not pretending. It's more like an internship."

"Mom and dad would be so proud of your career trajectory. First you drop out of college and now you're Chad the Intern?"

"Tell and I'll fucking kill you."

Chad took some codeine before the party, to see what it was like. Andrel picked him up and they crossed the bridge into Council Bluffs.

"I've got a sheet of acid, divided into ten-strips," explained Andrel, as he pulled up in front of the house. "I can front you a couple to sell in ones and twos at the party for five bucks a hit."

"What do you think I can get for this codeine?"

"All you got is codeine? I was hoping you might have weed or meth. Shit these people actually want."

The house smelled like stale Cheetos. It was full of people. Chad followed Andrel upstairs to meet his friend who claimed he could score quaaludes. People lounged on dingy second-hand furniture, smoking cigarettes and having unhinged conversations.

"These people look like they could use some LSD," hinted Andrel, not so subtly.

Chad mixed and mingled with little success, until he met Belinda. She wanted two hits of acid but didn't have any money.

"I'm willing to barter," she said.

"The purpose of dealing drugs is making money," said Chad. "I can't be giving my stash away every time some girl offers a hand job."

"I'm not offering a hand job," said Belinda. "I want to suck you off. For acid."

Blowjobs were Chad's weakness. "It's a deal."

He gave her two tabs of acid. Little squares of white paper stamped with purple moons. Belinda was excited. She placed the acid on her tongue and waved her hands in the air like a disco dancer.

"I've never done acid before," she said. "What's it like?"

"The high is super clean and the visuals are spectacular," he said. "I took two hits of purple moons and my hands turned into massive pillars of cotton candy. I stared at them the whole trip."

"Sounds awesome," she said. "Ready to get your dick sucked?"

"This is weird," he said. "I don't even know you."

"My name's Belinda and I'm a Pisces," she offered a handshake. "My hobbies are roller derby and playing harmonica on street corners."

"Harmonica is an underrated instrument."

"Enough with the chit-chat. Can we get this over with?"

Belinda led Chad to the bathroom. The fixtures were relics of an era when pink toilets were popular. There were mirrors on the walls.

"How are we going to do this?"

"Stand on the toilet so I don't have to kneel. I've got bad knees."

Chad climbed up and took out his cock. There wasn't much to work with. His penis was small and grey, with the texture of a dried apricot. It looked like it wanted to hide beneath his overgrown matte of pubic hair.

Belinda tugged on his member, looking for signs of life. Chad couldn't feel a thing.

"I was hoping for a little enthusiasm," she said.

"I think I need a jumpstart."

Belinda took it into her mouth and rolled her tongue around the head.

"That's good," he said. "Keep doing that."

"It's not responding."

"Jesus Christ," he said. He was failing the internship. A strange woman wanted to suck his dick for acid and he couldn't get it up. "I'm a visual guy. Maybe if you take your tits out I can rise to the occasion."

"Only because I feel sorry for you."

Belinda took her top off. A ring of red lipstick circled Chad's limp cock. It looked like a sad clown who'd been banished from the circus.

"You've got great tits," he said.

"Thanks," she said. "And no, you can't have a feel."

She rolled her lips over her teeth and tugged on Chad's shaft. No response. His cock hung there like a deflated balloon. There was no point in continuing.

"It's not working," he said. "Probably because I took codeine earlier."

"Excuses, excuses."

Belinda covered herself up while Chad tucked his defective dong back into his trousers. It was an awkward situation, like being in an elevator full of strangers. There was no way to avoid eye contact aside from looking straight up at the ceiling.

"I traded you two hits of acid for a blowjob," he said. "The way I see it, since you were unable to finish me off, you still owe me a blowjob."

"I don't owe you shit," said Belinda. "It's not my fault you can't get it up."

"Maybe we can meet up this week," said Chad. "We can grab lunch at that new Mexican place, Señor Tata's. We can have some tacos, a pitcher of margaritas, and then go somewhere nice and cosy where you can finish the blowjob."

"Tacos and a blowjob," said Belinda. "How absolutely romantic."

"I actually like you. It could be like a date," he said. "You like tacos, right? Give me a chance and you might find I'm not such a bad guy."

"You make girls suck your dick for drugs," she said. "Most people would say you're a fucking sicko."

"But we had a deal. You owe me a blowjob," said Chad. "If you don't want to finish it later, how about you suck off my friend Andrel? He's in the next room."

This wasn't about a blowjob anymore, it was about Chad's integrity. The fantasy of tacos and romance were a distraction. He recalibrated his focus. What would the drug dealer playbook say? He needed to get his money's worth out of this failed transaction.

"You want me to suck your friend's cock? That's classic. Yeah, totally. Go get your friend and I'll suck him off. I'll even let you watch so you can see what you're missing."

Chad left Belinda in the bathroom and went to find Andrel. He was smoking a bowl with a group of long-haired hippie stoners. They were zoning out to a seventeen-minute prog rock bass solo. Drugs really did strange things to people.

"Dude, I got a situation here."

"What the hell are you talking about," said Andrel. "How can you get yourself into a situation with a few hits of acid and some codeine."

"I met a girl who wants to suck your dick," said Chad. "She's ready for it right now in the bathroom."

"Why don't you get your own dick sucked?"

"Long story. Just let her give you a blowjob," pleaded Chad. "It would really help me out."

"Why do I feel like I'm going to regret this?"

Belinda was clever enough not to stick around. The bathroom was empty. The acid was already in her system, the visuals kicking in. Her arms had probably transformed into pillars of cotton candy by now. Andrel sat on the toilet as Chad confessed to his ineptitude.

"Chad, you let that girl play you," he said. "What does the drug dealer playbook say about that? Always get scratch. You know what scratch is?"

"Cash. Real money."

"What else does the drug dealer playbook say?"

"Never get high on your own supply."

There was a bizarre quality to the moment. The pink toilet. Belinda. Purple moons. The unfinished blowjob. The codeine. Geraldine's wisdom teeth. Images that hung like fog in Chad's consciousness. So many questions to ponder. Was he supposed to assign some deeper meaning, or was he simply living out another directionless night in his directionless life?

"Look, I appreciate your enthusiasm," said Andrel. "But we need to deal with the fact that you're not cut out for dealing drugs."

"You're terminating my internship?"

"This isn't a Fortune 500 company. We don't have interns. Selling drugs isn't for square corporate America types. There's no CEO. We don't have a 401K. There's no stock options in the dope game."

The codeine hit Chad all at once. It slowed things down, like a VHS cassette advancing frame by frame, unravelling in zapruderian detail.

"I wasn't at my best tonight," sighed Chad. "I'm pretty sure it's the codeine."

"Look at yourself. You've got parents that love you. You sell drugs like an idiot but you've got book smarts," said Andrel. "You should go back to school. Get a high-paying job in the global financial sector. Move to Hong Kong. Buy a fucking jet-ski."

"Hong Kong?" said Chad. "A jet-ski?"

"I don't know, move anywhere in the fucking world. My point is, don't put limitations on your future. Harness that potential of yours. Be somebody."

Andrel was right. He should go back to college and put his nose to the grindstone, like his old man used to say. Make something of himself. A college degree would be the logical next step, but something inside him seemed defective. He seemed hardwired to make stupid decisions. How was this supposed to change?

Geraldine was still up when he got home, watching Jerry Springer on basic cable. She looked chipmunkish from the post-surgical swelling.

"You look like shit," said Chad. He tossed a blister pack her way. "Have some codeine."

Geraldine washed down the pills with apple juice.

"Mister big-shot drug dealer couldn't move a little codeine," she said dryly. "Have you considered that you might not be cut out for the dope game?"

"The internship is over," Chad said. "Andrel gave me a spiel about how he 'appreciates my enthusiasm' and cut me loose."

"That's what you say when someone's shit at their job."

"I'm aware."

Chad sat down on the couch next to his sister. It seemed like forever since the two of them watched trashy television together. He was hit with a wave of nostalgia for Degrassi Junior High reruns and cheesy after school specials.

"What's Chad the Intern's next move?"

Tough question. He didn't know. He would handle it like he handled everything else, by winging it. Making up the rules as he went along. Andrel's pep talk made a lot of sense, especially the part about moving to Hong Kong and getting a jet-ski.

"I guess it's back to school for me," he said. "I was shit at dealing drugs, but something tells me I might make a good pharmacist."

NICHE INTEREST

Newly-certified scuba diver Turk Blanchard completed a textbook giant stride into the seapool of the abandoned Mar-a-Loco Resort. He added two sharp blasts of air to his BCD and rolled onto his back for the long kick-out to Staghorn Point, a popular shore dive site on the tropical island of Grand Calabash.

The PADI manual frowned on solo diving, but Turk had a specific mission in mind. A dive buddy was unlikely to share his niche interest.

If something goes wrong, a dive buddy probably won't save me anyway. A diver needs to learn self-reliance. Risk is inherent, it's how you manage risk that makes you a competent diver.

Just getting to the seapool was an adventure. Turk parked along the perimeter of the old resort. He fed his dive gear through a cut in the chain link fence and dragged it on hands and knees underneath a thicket of sea-grape trees. He crossed the rubble patch where the tiki bar used to be, then down the crumbling concrete steps to crystal-clear waters of the Caribbean Sea. This man-made harbour is where Mar-a-Loco housed their dive vessels, before Hurricane Norma wiped out the island's north side.

The trek was worth it, conditions were perfect. The surface was calm and flat, with unlimited visibility underneath. Staghorn Point was about two hundred meters offshore. Turk kicked out to the marker buoy and descended. The top of the mini-wall was around 40 feet. He slowly cruised down the gentle slope, following a groove in the reef banked with sea fans and coral pillars.

This place looks like the centrefold in one of those scuba magazines. I used to think scuba diving was an bizarre hobby, but now it's my way of life. I'm a certified open water diver in beautiful Grand Calabash with world-class coral reefs at my doorstep. And it's only gonna get better when I find the Sponge Belt.

Staghorn Point was teeming with fish. Massive schools of grunts and jacks clustered restlessly in the shade of looming coral bommies. Filefish couples slow-danced above vast thickets of staghorn coral, entrancing each other with their amorous displays of colour. The lippy underbite of a goliath grouper jutted from underneath an overhang. Turk reached the sandy flats, 64 feet deep according to his Suunto dive computer, like a hockey puck strapped to his wrist.

Turk followed the sand channel as it weaved through a maze of coral fingers towards the main wall. He was looking for a spot the locals called the Sponge Belt. His Suunto read 98 feet at the drop-off. Beyond was the abyss. The Calabash trench was one of the deepest on the planet, more than a mile deep. When something went that far down, there was no coming back.

I wonder what it would be like to swim out into total blueness, to be swallowed up in it, what a thrill that would be. To lose all concept of what's up and what's down, alone in the vast ocean. How humbling that would be. It would also be really fucking stupid, considering I'd probably drift to Honduras in the current.

Turk's air was at 2000psi, enough to spend five or ten minutes at the Sponge Belt, depending on air consumption. Plenty of time to accomplish his objective. Finding his way back would be the tricky part. First to the mini-wall, then the Mar-a-Loco seapool. He'd be fucked if he lost his bearings.

Cross that bridge when you get there, the most important thing is to find the Sponge Belt, to do what you came here to do. A competent scuba diver must overcome adversity to execute the mission.

Turk was hunting a species of dwarf tube sponge he'd seen in a nature documentary. Over millions of years, this particular sponge developed a symbiotic relationship with the elusive windmill shrimp. The documentary showed the windmill shrimp using its feathery appendages to brush parasites from visiting fish, who seemed to find the experience quite satisfying.

Turk found the underwater footage extremely arousing. The fantasy of experiencing the services of the windmill shrimp for his own gratification inspired him to change his life. Not only did he take up the expensive hobby of scuba diving, he abandoned life in the big city to move to Grand Calabash, one of three places in the Caribbean where windmill shrimp were known to exist.

Turk located a colony of dwarf tube sponges. They looked like something out of a Dr. Seuss fever dream. Variegated structures, whimsically shaped, in shocking hues of orange and green. The sponge was a tiny apartment tower for the windmill shrimp. A cluster of dwarf tube sponges had attached itself to the arm of a cactus-shaped coral, at the perfect height to pursue his fucked-up fantasy.

Technically, this is bestiality. But the shrimp is only following its instinct. It doesn't know any better. To the shrimp my dong is just another fish. It gets a meal out of my dead skin cells and whatnot and doesn't know it's being exploited for my sexual gratification. We're just two animals in the same vast ocean, interwoven into the fabric of nature.

Turk looked both ways for the bubbles of other divers. When satisfied he was alone, he undid his board shorts. He pulled out his cock, which already throbbed with anticipation. He barged past a red squirrelfish and waggled his prick at the mouth of the sponge. This motion, he learned from the documentary, was a signal to the windmill shrimp that a client was in need of his services.

Come on out, you beautiful little shrimp. My one-eyed trouser eel needs your feathery appendages to rid its girth of parasites. I'm so fucking horny right now, I can't wait to empty my balls all over this reef.

A pair of windmill shrimp emerged from the sponge and went to work. They were translucent, with a thin blue stripe on their bodies. One worked Turk's head and shaft, the other concentrated on the balls, windmilling its appendage with a titillating bit of pressure to his scrotal sack.

This feels even better than I expected. Keep going you sexy little fuckers, yeah, just like that. Right there, oh yes. Holy shit, I'm gonna bust my nut.

Turk's cock hiccuped a ropey cloud of jizz into the water. It startled the windmill shrimp. They retracted their appendages and darted back to the safety of their sponge hotel.

Please come back! I was hoping for some after-play.

He squeezed the last drops out of his cock and tucked it back into his board shorts. What a comedown from the towering heights of ecstasy. Thanks to the windmill shrimp, he'd had the most powerful orgasm of his life. He checked his air gauge. All that heavy breathing had left him just below 1000psi. The realisation that he was 98 feet deep on the edge of the abyss was sobering. He needed to start his ascent now, so he could burn off nitrogen before surfacing.

Whatever happens, make sure you don't get the bends. That's the last thing you need. How embarrassing would it be to show up bent at the bariatric chamber needing treatment? Jesus Christ, how much would a chamber ride cost? Could I be stripped of my PADI certification for my recklessness?

It was a situation Turk hoped to avoid. He frog kicked towards shore as he ascended at a slow but steady pace. The plan was to stay high in the water column to conserve air. He cruised over the sand flats at a depth of 25 feet, peering down at the reef. A pair of eagle rays snorted into the sand, hunting for hidden molluscs. Massive schools of blue tang steamrolled over the coral fingers, picking bits of algae off the seafloor. A free-swimming moray eel poked his head into the critter holes under a ledge. Turk took another reading of his air gauge.

Fucking shit. I'm at 400psi and not even back to the mini-wall. Am I even going the right way? I can't tell from up here if this is the same sand channel I followed out. Jesus Christ, what a nightmare. Maybe I should've brought a compass, not that I would remember how to use it under pressure.

The Suunto beeped when Turk hit safety-stop depth. The weather had taken a turn for the worse since he kicked out. The surface churned above him and the sky was fluorescent grey. Three minutes here and he would be safe to surface, in theory.

The weatherman said nothing about thunderstorms on the north shore. This is either a pop-up storm, a random weather fluke, or karma is seriously fucking with me. Am I a monster for using the coral reef as my personal jack-off device?

He detected a flash of lightning through the surface chop and felt the muted rumble of thunder. Raindrops danced on the water's surface. From below they looked like tiny diamonds, sparkling amidst the wave action.

I'm going to run out of air and I'll have to kick back to Mar-a-Loco through this shit. What a fucking disaster. I could get struck by lighting. All because of my desire to molest the marine life. I really am a sick fuck.

Turk sucked at his regulator. His tank was close to empty and it took mammoth effort to extract even the tiniest breath. His gauge tipped to below zero. He gave his BCD his last blast of air and bobbed to the surface, gasping to fill his lungs.

Turk's vantage point was demoralising. 200 yards is a long way when you're exhausted, out of air, and facing a surface swim through pummelling rain and choppy seas. He struggled to stay above the water, as if an invisible hand was pulling him down by the valve of his tank. Even worse, his BCD, the device keeping him afloat, was gurgling and hissing— a telltale sign of a slow leak.

This wouldn't be happening if I owned my own scuba gear. I thought the dive shop would check for leaks before they sent out equipment with a customer. I never should've trusted this shitty rental equipment, it's going to get me killed. Why do I have to be such a fucking cheapskate?

Turk reached behind himself, and with considerable effort located the manual inflation tube for his BCD. Timing his breath in the persistent chop was difficult. The waves slapped his face at every opportunity. He took on a mouthful of seawater and nearly choked, but regained his composure. He was faintly aware he was drifting off-course from the abandoned Mar-a-Loco resort.

The main thing is getting back to shore. There's a beach over there. I can swim to it, find my way through the casuarina trees back to the road, and follow it back to the resort. A new twist on the walk of shame.

The kick-in was excruciating. He took the pockets out of his rental BCD and dumped the weights onto the hardpan. Eight fewer pounds of lead to carry. The BCD continued to gurgle, losing air. Turk worked out a rhythm, kicking hard and taking big steady breaths to feed his quads with fresh air. He could feel the accumulated nitrogen in his bloodstream boiling off, like champagne in his veins. After what seemed like hours of kicking, he arrived at a scraggy strip of undeveloped Grand Calabash beach.

This land would be a goldmine for a Real Estate developer who knows the right politicians' hands to shake. The way it's going, this place is gonna be totally destroyed within a decade. A concrete jungle, indeed. Foreign developers are ruining Grand Calabash's rustic island charm.

Turk slipped out of his fins to negotiate the exit. The surf bullied him with constant knockdown waves as he struggled on his back like an overturned turtle. Finally he extricated himself from the latches and straps that secured the tank and BCD to his body. He dragged himself up the beach, scraping his thigh on beach rock protruding from sugar-white sand. Finally, he was out of the water.

He collapsed in the powdery sand that fringed the high-water mark and looked out at the choppy sea. Bobbing in the spume were his bright orange rental fins, taunting him from out in the chop.

No way. I'm not going back out there into that mess, not without fins. It's probably 20 feet deep out there in the hardpan. I'll just pay whatever the fee is for losing the fins. Another kick in the face for Mr. Cheapskate. When will I ever learn?

He hoisted his tank and BCD onto his back and trudged through the scrubby underbrush. This area was designated to become a national park decades before, but that project became snarled in the gears of the political machine. Another brilliant idea shot to shit in the morass of Calabash politics. The land, used by locals as an illegal dumpsite, was criss-crossed by a maze of pothole-ridden marl roads, infested with hissing green iguanas and bloodthirsty swamp mosquitos.

Turk found a road and followed it. Rivulets of watery blood ran down his leg, from inside his board shorts. He felt a burning sensation on his thigh from where he scraped himself on beach rock. As the saltwater air dried on his body, the lining of his board shorts chafed against his undercarriage. Mosquitos crawled all over him, feeding at will. He couldn't swat them away because his hands were full of scuba equipment, which got heavier with each fork in the marl road.

By the time he hit the paved road, Turk was exhausted. His Pajero was at the crest of the hill, parked under a streetlight along the Mar-a-Loco perimeter fence. After everything he'd been through, the last bit looked impossibly far. His back ached from extra weight of his tank and BCD.

I deserve a big fat steak dinner after what I've been through. A hot bath, a cold six pack. Have a laugh about how I cheated death. I'm a lucky fucking bastard.

Turk reached the Pajero. He loaded the rental equipment into the boot, covered himself with an oversize beach towel, and discreetly executed a roadside change.

He wiggled out of his wet clothes, dabbed at the scrapes on his thigh, and wiped saltwater residue from his sticky body. His calves and ankles were polka-dotted with mosquito bites. He indulged himself with a scratch before towelling off his sea-salted cock and balls.

He opened the driver door. The seats of his Pajero were gone. Scrapyard scoundrels taking advantage of a scuba diver. Plenty of time to unbolt them and haul them away. Ordinary crackheads would've taken everything, the maps in the glove box, the coins in the ashtray, his Thin Lizzy Live and Dangerous CD. That stuff was chump change. The real money was in pre-owned auto parts.

I'll be forced to buy my own seats back from whatever scrapyard they turn up at. They'll act sympathetic, give me some line about how we paid good money for these, and that a business needs to cover its margins. These bastards are gonna extort me for a couple hundred bucks— for my own property. This island can go fuck itself sometimes.

Turk climbed into his seatless Pajero. He situated his buttocks on the floor, wedging them between the mounting brackets. It was a tight fit. Operating the pedals was not a problem, but he could barely see the road over the dashboard. The ride was neither safe or comfortable, but Turk made it to the booze shop, then home.

Turk stepped into the shower and cracked an Ironstone. A full-throated bock, weighing in at 7.5%

alcohol, Ironstone was the best bang for the buck in the Calabash Islands, where cheap beer was nonexistent.

The beer was cold and went down easy. Turk finished the bottle in one protracted swig and lathered himself. The scapes on his thigh stung as he dabbed at them with the soapy washcloth. He then moved on to armpits, elbows, knees, and feet. His last stop was his undercarriage, which had started to burn. Turk dropped the washcloth in shock.

Stinging cells, like jellyfish or fire coral. I should've known those fucking shrimp would have some sort of mechanism to thwart predators. Otherwise every Tom, Dick, and Harry with a PADI card would be down at the Sponge Belt getting their lance waxed. I'm such an idiot, such a fucking pervert. A sick shrimp-fucker. I really stuck my cock into trouble this time. What am I going to tell the doctor? This is so fucked up.

Raised red welts, like the stitches on a baseball, tracked across his cock and balls. Golden pus oozed from the lesions. Turk had been a victim of bad luck before, like when he picked up a dose of gonorrhoea on holiday in Ibiza. Another time he got chlamydia from a girl he hooked up with at a music festival. Then there was the time he caught crabs from a toilet seat, but that could've happened to anyone.

This time was different. Turk couldn't pin this on bad luck. He only had himself and his fucked up niche interest to blame.

NOBODY'S SUING ANYBODY HERE

Mom was back in town and desperate to reconnect after two years apart. It was strange though, so many things had changed. I wasn't a little kid anymore and she found it triggering to see me express my individuality through my hairstyle and clothing.

Maybe it was a shock for her to see me like this, with blue hair and a black trench-coat, but she needs to understand I'm sixteen years old now, capable of making my own decisions without her well-intentioned guidance.

I wasn't comfortable at her new house. I tried to avoid going there, instead scheduling our 'precious mother-daughter time' for bistro lunches and trips to the shopping mall. I do enjoy spending time with her, but I prefer to avoid her husband Barry whenever possible. He's unemployed and always home in his bathrobe, stinking up the bathroom with his medical cannabis. What a chode!

When Mom invited the whole family over for a 4th of July barbecue, my luck ran out. She caught me off-guard and I didn't have an excuse ready.

"You're so artistic, sweetie," she said. "I'm sure you'll make the most amazing place cards for our guests."

I got roped into helping her with party preparations. It's in Mom's nature to overdo things. I arrogantly thought my presence might be a calming influence.

"It's only a barbecue," I told her. "Not tea with the queen."

Saying no to Mom is entirely difficult. She does this sympathy trick, looking at me with her pathetic motherly eyes, and then the tears flow. When she cries, I start crying, and eventually we end up in the kitchen spooning raw cookie dough into our puffy-eyed crying faces. And somehow, Mom gets her way. It's kind of like her superpower.

When she asked if I would help out with the barbecue, it was like an out-of-body experience. I floated there, powerlessly, watching myself say yes.

"That's great, pumpkin," said Mom.

She moved in for a hug but I ducked it. "Mom, can we not do this today?"

"Do what today?"

"This charade," I said. "Pretending we have a normal relationship."

Preparations included an evening of baking. Mom assured me Barry the chode would be in his man-cave watching Deadliest Catch and not strutting around the house in his disgusting bathrobe. We made dozens of cupcakes and apple fritters. Mom, always the overachiever, insisted we make everything from scratch.

"What would Aunt Liz say if she found out I used a box recipe," she said. Sometimes Mom was funny. "She would have heart palpitations."

I threw out a test. "Aunt Liz can fuck herself."

Mom is so predictable. She gasped when I said the F-word, but Mom was also capable of surprises.

"The judgemental old cunt," she said, completely deadpan. "I sometimes feel like calling her that to her face. Always looking down on our side of the family like she's some rare pearl."

"Mom, the c-word," I gasped. "Jesus Christ."

"Who's the prude now?" she laughed. "If you want to start swearing around your Mom, you'll need to grow a thicker skin."

Aside from doing the washing up it was actually really fun hanging out with Mom. Maybe things were getting better between us. I actually started to look forward to the barbecue.

It started off like every other family gathering. Awkward hugs with aunts and uncles and catching up with cousins you barely remembered. A bunch of people standing around a table piled high with chips and dip and platters of meat and cheese rolled into cigarillos. Drinking and uncomfortable laughter as a group of people linked loosely by common DNA made small-talk and looked for an opportunity to make an early exit.

When fireworks rolled around everybody seemed pretty drunk. Mom and Uncle Wallace were telling old stories about sneaking out as teenagers, stealing bottles of vodka from my grandparents' liquor cabinet and throwing up on the stairs.

Barry was embarrassing himself, as usual. He was heavily self-medicated, as evidenced by his bloodshot eyes, dressed in a red, white, and blue three-piece suit bedazzled in sequins. "Fireworks are ready, everybody! Freshen up your drinks and gather in the backyard for the amazing spectacle!"

Spectacle was an overstatement. The fireworks were purchased in a package deal. The first ones stayed close to the ground. They had names like 'tears of a clown' and 'showering medusa.' When the fuses were lit they whistled and popped and sent showers of colourful sparks into the air. The display progressed onto bigger and bigger explosions until it was time for the grand finale.

"This one's called the omega-plasmatron." Barry loved the sound of his own voice and clearly revelled in having a captive audience. "Sixteen larger-than-life bursts of colour will soon illuminate the night sky. It's a Chinese-made homage to the patriots of 1776 and a fitting testament to the American spirit and its two-and-a-half centuries of reliance on imported goods and labour."

"Enough with American History 101," interjected Uncle Wallace. "Just light the goddamn thing."

Barry leaned in with a cigarette lighter. The fuse hissed and the grand finale was underway. The omega-plasmatron was incredibly loud and unnervingly close. Each explosion sent a grapefruit-sized projectile full of Chinese gunpowder into the sky where it burst into a dazzling sphere of colour.

It was so embarrassing. I mean, no wonder people in other countries think Americans are idiots. We blow things up for entertainment.

Something went wrong. The oohs and aaahs turned to panicked shrieks. The omega-plasmatron toppled onto its side and was shooting exploding grapefruits right at us. I didn't have time to think or scream. There was a flash, then a hot rush of air whooshed past my face. Before I knew what was happening my hair was on fire.

Everyone screamed, then the world went silent, like it does for dramatic effect in those insufferable art movies. I smelled gunpowder. Huge clumps of blue hair fell out in my hands. I was having a panic attack. Mom whisked me into the bathroom to calm me down.

She sat me on the toilet and went through my roots, looking for smouldering embers on my scalp. It reminded me of second grade when they sent me home with a letter about headlice. The fine-toothed comb they used to prise the eggs from the shafts of individual hairs. The way the medicated shampoo burned my scalp. How I cried in the bathtub, feeling ashamed and sorry for myself.

"You've definitely been hit." Mom was crying. "Oh sweetie, this is all my fault."

"Don't be like this," I told her. "This isn't anybody's fault."

"It's Barry's fault. You could probably sue the fat prick for gross negligence," said cousin Jessica, the law student. "The instructions said to partially bury the omega-plasmatron in the ground before you light the fuse. There's no way that douche canoe did that."

"Nobody's suing anybody here," said Mom. "It was just an accident, a rite of passage. How badass will it be to add a firework disaster to your origin story."

The rest of the party was awful. Everyone was super nice to me, even Barry, who was profusely apologetic, but I'm pretty sure my hair on fire spoiled the barbecue for everyone.

Mom tries so hard to arrange nice things for the family, and somehow I find a way to ruin it with my drama. I locked myself inside the bathroom and cried. Clumps of singed hair were all over the counter. I gathered it up and stuffed it into my handbag.

I had to get out. There was nothing here for me anymore, in this so-called family. I texted my boyfriend and told him to meet me at the Metro station in ten minutes. I climbed over the toilet tank and out the bathroom window into the summer night.

I could see everything clearly. My next step, the steps after that, like an endless staircase in an MC Escher sketch. When I turn seventeen I'll move on from all this family bullshit. I'll shave off what's left of my hair and emerge from my chrysalis a completely different person. I will do it again and again, if I have to, until things get better.

SARATOGA 120'S

Bucky's Bagels was way out in the suburbs. Lucas Parnell had to be there at 4:30 AM to bake bagels for the morning rush. The hours were shit, but it was the only job he could get that paid more than minimum wage.

The alarm went off at 3:30. Lucas hit snooze twice before crawling out of bed and into his uniform, an Aloha-from-Hawaii era Elvis jumpsuit without rhinestones. There was no point in showering before an eight-hour shift standing at the mouth of a 500 degree stone oven. He yawned, rubbed the sleep out of his eyes, and scratched his balls. It was time to go to work.

It was a twenty minute drive from his cockroach-infested downtown apartment. The one benefit of an early morning commute was the absence of other traffic. He chain-smoked as he drove, drumming along to Superchunk on the steering wheel of his Subaru as he headed deep into the bowels of suburbia.

In times like these it felt like nicotine was the only thing keeping him going. Lucas was first to arrive for the morning shift. He lit another cigarette and waited for the others behind Bucky's Bagels. Audrey and Sheila showed up a few minutes later. They were easygoing college girls who never gave Lucas any trouble. They spread cream cheese on bagels and worked the cash register.

The three of them stood groggily waiting for Quincy, who was always late. The assistant manager, he was the only one trusted with a key to the building. Overweight and prematurely balding, he spent half the morning locked in a glorified closet he called an office drinking sugary coffee and watching SportsCentre on ESPN. The rest of his time was spent berating staff, complaining about the high cost of doing business, and making lewd remarks to his female underlings. A typical asshole.

Quincy's BMW pulled up, a typical car for a typical asshole.

"Morning, Quincy," Audrey and Sheila cooed.

"Sorry I'm late," he said, fumbling with his keys. "Had another great night at the greyhound track last night with my good buddy Johnny Walker Black. The winning streak won't quit, and neither will the hangover."

He unlocked the door and held it open for the college girls. Lucas puffed on his cigarette and scowled. He was keenly aware that Quincy's late arrival had cost him a quarter of an hour's pay.

"Are you gonna just stand there, or are you coming to work today?"

Lucas stubbed his cigarette out on his shoe and flicked it towards the dumpster. It was time to bake the bagels.

"I've been here fifteen minutes, are you going to pay me for that time?"

"I don't pay you to smoke, I pay you to make the fucking bagels. Get clocked-in, and get your ass to work."

It didn't take a Rhodes Scholar to master the trade. First, dough is formed into bagel-sized hoops and placed on trays in a large rack. Then the bagels are boiled in a large vat of barley malt for two or three minutes until they float to the surface. The floating bagels are scooped out of the bubbling malt and placed five at a time on narrow metal skids. The skids are then placed into the 500 degree oven. Plain bagels go straight in. Flavoured bagels are dusted with an assortment of herbs and spices before going in. The bagels bake in the stone hearth for precisely five minutes, any more or less and they're rejected as unsellable. The golden-brown bagels are then removed from the oven and placed in the appropriate wire basket for that particular type of bagel. When a new batch arrived it was Lucas' responsibility to cheerfully announce the arrival of fresh bagels to the eager queue of Bucky's Bagels customers.

"Fresh pumpernickel bagels!" he bellowed when a new batch tumbled into the basket. "Fresh cinnamon raisin bagels! Get 'em while they're hot!"

Lucas stayed in constant motion during the morning rush, scooping, sprinkling, and maintaining a steady flow of fresh bagels to the sales counter.

There was a certain performative aspect to the job, which he supposed came along with the Elvis jumpsuit. Large windows surrounded his work station area so customers could observe the bagel-making process. Lucas danced to hits from the 60's and 70's as he baked, lip-syncing familiar lyrics into the mop handle, mugging through the glass at the dreary businessmen who stopped in for bagels and cream cheese before their morning sales meetings. Lucas burnt his forearms from time to time reaching into the stone hearth, but life wasn't so bad with the radio on.

The morning rush lasted until about 10:30. During the lull, Quincy popped out of his office to check the day's receipts and play grab-ass with Audrey and Sheila.

"You girls are way too pretty for college," he said. "What you need is to find yourselves rich husbands and squeeze out a couple kids. You'll be set for life and you'll never have to lift a finger."

Audrey and Sheila rolled their eyes and exchanged grimaces. They worked at Bucky's Bagels for the same reason Lucas did. It was the only fast food place that paid more than minimum wage. They tolerated a certain amount of his chauvinism but drew a hard line at physical harassment.

"If only we could be so lucky," Audrey swooned patronisingly. "Don't you have any rich and good-looking friends you can introduce us to?"

"One day our Prince Charming will sweep us off our feet and rescue us from Bucky's Bagels," said Shiela. "Until then, keep your filthy little sausage-fingers off our asses."

Quincy blushed red and retreated to his office. The girls high-fived. Mission accomplished.

Lucas tidied up his work station, mopping spilled barley malt from the floor and wiping granules of bagel toppings from the countertop. He popped his head into Quincy's office to announce his smoke break.

"Everything's clean and I'm all caught up," he said. "I'm popping out for a smoke."

Lucas sat on an overturned milk crate and lit his cigarette. The cherry glowed bright orange as he inhaled. It felt good to sit down and fill his lungs with nicotine after six hours on his feet. It wasn't fair. Quincy sat in a comfortable leather chair all day, drinking coffee and watching TV while Lucas busted his ass in front of that goddamn oven.

He checked his watch. He'd only been outside for five minutes. Plenty of time for another cigarette before going back to work. Only two hours left before he was free to do whatever he wanted with the rest of the day. He took a long drag, held it momentarily, then exhaled.

Quincy burst through the back door, red faced and arms flailing.

"What did I tell you, Parnell?" he said. "I don't pay you to smoke, I pay you to make the fucking bagels."

"I told you I was going out for a smoke."

"That's your second cigarette," he screeched. "I'm watching your ass on CCTV. You said you were going out for a smoke. Singular, not plural. Can we both agree that two is more than one?"

Lucas looked away at the dumpster. What did it matter if he smoked one cigarette or two cigarettes? A guy deserved a break once in awhile.

"A smoke is a figure of speech, not a precise unit of measurement," said Lucas. "I've only been out here for five minutes. Labour law entitles workers to two fifteen-minute breaks per eight-hour shift."

"The labour law is nothing but liberal left-wing propaganda," said Quincy, slipping into rhetoric drilled into him over a lifetime of exposure to conservative radio talking points. "Do you think America became the greatest country in the world by coddling its labour force?"

"I thought America was based on the rule of law."

"Exactly. He who haveth the money maketh the laws," Quincy's fat face twisted into a maniacal smile. "Now get your raggedy ass back in there and get some everything bagels prepped for the lunch rush."

Quincy slammed the door and left Lucas to snub out his cigarette. When he sauntered back to the baking station, Audrey and Sheila noticed he wasn't his happy-go-lucky self. The shop was empty so they joined him by the malt vat for a first-hand account of the workplace drama.

"What happened out there?"

"Typical douchebaggery. What we've come to expect from the asshole-in chief," Lucas tossed rings of bagel dough one by one into the boiling malt.

"What's that loser on about this time?"

"He says I'm only allowed one cigarette on my smoke break."

"That's ridiculous," said Audrey. "The poster in his office says we're all entitled to two fifteen-minute breaks per eight-hour shift."

"Quincy doesn't give a fuck about labour law," Lucas shook his head. "He went old testament on me, saying he who haveth the money maketh the laws. He told me to get my ass in here and bake some fucking bagels."

"I've got an idea that will really fuck with that asshole," said Sheila. "My Aunt Lorraine smoked these long brown cigarettes called Saratoga 120's. They come in a faux-ostrich skin pack. You should get a pack of Saratogas for when you go on break. It took her at least a half-hour to smoke one down to the filter."

"A half-hour for one cigarette?"

"She had a Saratoga in her hand in literally all of my childhood photographs."

"Hedy Lamar used to smoke Saratogas," offered Audrey. "So did Greta Garbo."

"Sounds glamorous," said Lucas. "Maybe I'll give them a try."

"You should. It would really fuck with that fat piece of shit. I really hate him with a passion."

If anyone deserved fucking with, it was Quincy. Lucas stopped at Kum-n-Go on the way home and bought two packs of Saratoga 120's. They were an uncool brand marketed at old ladies, but he didn't give a fuck about his image. All he cared about was getting one over on his asshole boss. The nicotine was just a bonus.

He unwrapped the cellophane and pulled a Saratoga from its faux ostrich-skin package. The filter and paper were chocolatey brown, delineated by two gold lamé bands. The word 'Saratoga' was embossed in flamboyant cursive on the shaft of the cigarette, also in gold lamé. Lucas could see why Hedy Lamar would choose Saratogas, they were devilishly glamorous.

The next morning was a rerun of the day before. Quincy arrived late, full of braggadocio about his triumphs at the greyhound track. Audrey and Sheila sidestepped his wandering hands and parried his misogynistic remarks. Meanwhile, Lucas kept Bucky's stocked with fresh bagels.

"Fresh garlic and onion bagels!" he shouted. "Fresh blueberry bagels!"

After the morning rush Lucas took a seat on a milk crate and lit up a Saratoga 120. For a so-called old lady cigarette it was robust and flavourful. He rested his aching feet as he puffed and puffed at the monster cigarette. As promised, the Saratoga burnt long and strong.

Predictably, Quincy burst through the back door in a rage. "I don't pay you to smoke, I pay you to make the fucking bagels. Did we not discuss the cigarette break policy yesterday?"

"I'm following the policy. You said I'm permitted one cigarette on my break." Lucas checked his watch. "I lit this bad boy exactly twenty-three minutes ago and I've still got half a cigarette left. Check the CCTV if you don't believe me."

"Cut the shit, Parnell," snapped Quincy. "People want hot, fresh bagels right fucking now. We're running low on poppyseed bagels. It's fucking bedlam in there."

"I don't maketh the rules, I just adhereth to them," Lucas took a massive drag on his Saratoga and blew smoke rings at his boss. "I'll get back to work after I finish this delicious and refreshing cigarette."

Quincy stormed away, slamming the door behind him. Audrey and Sheila were geniuses. The Saratoga trick had really fucked with their asshole boss. Lucas smiled and took another drag, relishing the sense of satisfaction that came from sticking it to the man. His job was safe for the time being, but as soon as Quincy found a new underling to bake the bagels he'd be cut loose.

Lucas didn't give two shits about Bucky's Bagels anyway. A job was a job and there was always another one lurking around the corner. In that moment there was only Lucas and his Saratoga 120, so long and elegant he thought he might go on smoking it forever.

HE THOUGHT HE WAS HOT SHIT

Trevor carried himself like a tropical macaw, flamboyantly coiffed and dripping with brylcreem, draped in a Hawaiian shirt. He had customised his second-hand leather jacket, adding punk rock studs and spikes plus the logo of his band, the Ice Cream Socialists, on the back.

He carried a toothpick in his teeth, maintaining a nonconformist sneer as he strode into the afterparty, thirsty for beer and a warm body to get off with later when he was banjaxed on cheap beer. Trevor was the drummer in a punk rock band. He thought he was hot shit.

The party house was packed with punks and the punk-adjacent: weirdos, shifty-eyed geeks, and militant vegans. Most he recognised from the local scene, but there were some fresh faces too. The keg was in the kitchen, but so was his ex-girlfriend Stacey. Trevor made an about-face when he heard her cackling laughter and ended up in the backyard, where a group of punk rockers drank beer and tossed the empties into a budding bonfire.

"If you see any wood lying around, bring it over," shouted an attractive blue-haired girl Trevor didn't recognise. A giant bullring dangled from her pierced septum. "Let's burn this motherfucker down!"

"There's some wooden chairs in the kitchen," said Trevor manipulating his toothpick suggestively. "Come get a beer with me and we can take the chairs and smash them up. Let's burn this motherfucker down!"

"You're the drummer from Ice Cream Socialists, aren't you?" said the blue-haired girl, who introduced herself as Kim. She fluttered her eyelids, which took much effort and stamina, owing to her massive fake eyelashes. "You guys were crisp, too legit to quit. In other words, you were fucking right-on. I was there to see Jupiter Biscotti, but you guys blew them off stage."

Trevor soaked up the complement, wagging his toothpick like a labradoodle's nubby tail. He turned on a performative faux-modesty he had been practicing for exactly this occasion.

"Wow, thanks. Jupiter Biscotti were, I mean, are, an amazing band. Their early stuff was a big influence on the Ice Cream Socialists when we got started. They lost some of the magic when Greg left and they got that atrocious new singer…"

"My ex-boyfriend."

"The atrocious new singer— no fucking way!"

"I wouldn't call it the biggest mistake of my life, but he's somewhere in the top ten. You know how small town punk scenes are basically incestuous cesspools? If you break up with somebody you'll see them at every party, and they'll probably be fucking one of your friends in a few weeks. Me and him are still friends, nominally, mainly because we run in the same circles."

"I totally understand. My ex-girlfriend is here, in the kitchen, hanging around like a stale fart."

"Is she that redhead with the terrible laugh?" Kim covered her face with a hand to suppress her own laughter, which wasn't exactly chamber music.

"That's the one," he said, making a face like a toddler who has just eaten his first lemon. "Total psycho."

"I don't think she's taking the breakup well. I overheard her commiserating with her squad, the wine-girl-weekend posse."

"What did she say?"

"I think the words she used were, 'the boy's got oral skills galore, an average cock, and he's a terrible narcissist.' She also told a rather entertaining but unflattering story about you."

"Which one?"

"The fact that you have more than one is unsettling."

"I believe in living exuberantly. She wasn't telling the one about when I sprayed whipped cream on my cock at a party, and let a bunch of kittens lick it off?"

"Dude, that's fucking twisted," she kicked him in the shin. "You don't fuck with kittens, man, it's technically bestiality."

"So it wasn't that one."

"No," she folded her arms across her chest. "But I need an explanation. What the actual fuck?"

"The whipped cream and the kittens weren't my idea. I was in a phase where I liked taking my cock out at parties and getting reactions."

"Perfectly reasonable behaviour," she said. "For a pervert."

"It was just a phase. Like wearing suspenders back when ska was popular."

"I can't stand ska unless it's first wave."

"You've got great taste."

Trevor twirled his toothpick seductively, end over end with considerable skill. It had a hypnotising effect on Kim, who was beginning to melt from the centre. She felt the moist heat in her steampunk underwear.

"My ex's assessment of my oral skills is astute. I do, however, take umbrage with her methodology when coming to an 'average' cock rating. If girth were taken into account, I'm sure I would qualify as an average plus."

"I like girth."

"Are we flirting?"

"No, you're explaining why you let innocent kittens lick whipped cream off your cock. You just revealed that you're the kind of sicko that likes to wave his pickle around at parties."

"Like I said, it was a phase. I was drunk, just broke up with a different ex, and thought if I whipped it out then the girl of my dreams might like what was on offer and then we could live happily ever after."

"So you're looking for miss right."

"More like miss right now."

"Fair enough."

"When the whipped cream canister was empty, a few of us went into the bathroom to wash up, and ended up in a four-way fuck-fest. It was wild, getting buck naked in the shower with my best friend and two girls we went to high school with."

"Is this the same best friend, who's grandmother you gave the crabs?"

"Stacey told that story?"

"You gave a septuagenarian a sexually transmitted infection?"

"It didn't happen the way you think."

"Let me guess— she got it from a toilet seat?"

"I got kicked out of my parents house and went to stay at my best friend's house until things calmed down."

"Why did you get kicked out?"

"My dad found my weed stash. He's a cop and didn't take it well."

"Fucking hell."

"Exactly. So I'm staying in the guest room at my best friend's house, and I discover an entire colony of tiny crustaceans crawling around my undercarriage. Of course I panicked because I don't know if I got them from suspect A or suspect B."

"A love triangle," said Kim. "Ever identify the culprit?"

"I have my suspicions, but neither one admitted to it," Trevor paused to rearrange the toothpick in his teeth. "So, I go to the pharmacy and they give me a medicinal shampoo and a special comb designed to strip the eggs that had attached themselves to the pubes. In a few days, everything was back to normal."

"That still doesn't explain how you gave a 70-year-old woman crabs."

"So, my best friend's grandmother comes to town for a surprise visit and I was forced to vacate the guest bedroom. No one changed the sheets, which happened to be infested with crab eggs, and that explains how my best friend's grandmother caught crabs. From me, but only indirectly."

"He's still your best friend after that?"

"If anything, the experience brought us closer together. He absolutely detested that old bag and thought it was hilarious. But his parents connected the dots and I was banned from their house."

"Cool story, bro," said Kim. "Are you still serious about burning this motherfucker down? Let's get those fucking chairs."

"Fuck yeah, let's go!"

Kim pushed her way through the party to the kitchen, with Trevor in tow. His ex-girlfriend Stacey scowled. He felt giddy with satisfaction, knowing it burned her up to see him with another woman, especially so soon after the breakup. Stacey had a jealous streak. Kim sensed the dynamic and began a display of performative affection. She backed into him, placed his hands on her waist, and twisted her neck around to kiss him. He spat out the toothpick.

"Wowza," said Trevor, wiping the mollusc-like trail of goo left behind by her undulating lips. She really slimed him good. "Where did you learn that manoeuvre?"

"I'm free-styling."

It remained unspoken, but they were both acutely aware Trevor's boner was poking Kim in the kidney. His ex-girlfriend Stacey and her wine-girl-weekend posse were not impressed by the flagrant dry-hump unfolding before them. Kim rubbed her ample buttocks against Trevor's swollen dong like a baker kneading dough.

"Get a room, you two," interjected one of Stacey's plastic friends. "Nobody wants to see you going at it like baboons. Have some respect for your ex-girlfriend, and take your disgusting make-out session elsewhere."

It seemed a good time to leave as any. But there was still the matter of collecting fuel for the bonfire. Trevor pulled away from Kim and adjusted his cock, tucking it down his trouser-leg to deflate. The moment demanded he make an exit statement.

"On behalf of my average cock," he said, "I think it's best for Stacey and I to remain friends from a distance, and in the spirit of maturity and being the bigger person, Kim and I will politely fuck off."

"But first," interjected Kim. "We need your chairs."

"Get up," said Trevor, gesturing madly. "We only need two. Some of you could use some time on your feet. It helps sculpt the calves."

"Still a misogynist pig," said Stacey. "You never change, do you?"

Stacey's wine girls conferred, exchanged eye-rolls, and agreed to surrender two chairs to the cause of burning this motherfucker down.

Trevor winked and blew a kiss. "Stay classy, babe."

"Have a great night, you two," cackled Stacey, faking cheerfulness. "You deserve each other. By the way, he's a sexual gremlin. Don't let him drink whiskey after midnight or he won't be able to get it up."

"I have a feeling," winked Kim. "He'll get it up for me anytime I want."

Stacey groaned as Kim dragged Trevor from the kitchen by his ear. Stacey tried to control him, put him in a box, and almost succeeded. Ultimately Trevor was true to himself and broke free.

Kim burst through the door and onto the patio, holding a chair high above her head. Trevor followed close behind. Kim swung the chair by its back and smashed it into a brick wall several times until the wooden legs broke free from the seat.

"Annihilate these motherfuckers."

"Cowabunga!"

Trevor smashed his chair on the sidewalk, shattering its back legs and sending splinters of wood into his shins.

"Jesus suffering fuck," he shouted. "That fucking hurts."

Kim made a frowny-face and abruptly leaned in to kiss Trevor on the cheek. Her lips felt like marshmallows on his stubbled face.

"That was nice," he said.

"Don't forget the objective, horn-dog. You promised to help me burn this motherfucker down. Are we gonna burn this motherfucker down or what?"

"I need a minute to rest and recover."

"Rest and recovery isn't a punk rock concept. I thought you were supposed to be hot shit, with your hairdo, your Magnum PI shirt, and that leather jacket studded with ten million metallic doodads."

"Peer pressure isn't punk."

"You're wrong. Peer pressure is punk as fuck."

"And you're gonna pressure me to commit arson with you?"

"Whoa, hold up." Kim's demeanour changed. "You're getting lost in translation, Mr. McGirth. When I said let's burn the motherfucker down, I meant having the most badass bonfire ever, not criminal damage to property."

"Oh," said Trevor. "I feel kind of stupid now."

"You look pretty stupid," she pulled him towards her. "But stupid looking people can still redeem themselves. C'mon already— let's burn this motherfucker down."

Trevor gathered up the splintered chair wood and carried it to the bonfire. It was all beginning to make sense. Kim was hot for him, and he was hot for her. The bonfire was just an elaborate foreplay ritual. She gyrated her hips, waving hands above her head as Trevor chucked the chair legs into the blaze. The sappy wood crackled and popped like Rice Krispies in the flames.

"We need to step back," said Trevor. "Somebody might lose an eye."

"Lose an eye?"

"It happened to my grandfather when he was a boy. He was sitting at the fireplace with his big brother when a sap bubble popped. Embers shot out and hit both of them in the eye. My grandpa lost his right, his brother lost his left."

"Freak accident," she said. "That sounds pretty fucked up dude, but I need to keep on dancing. The heat of the fire feels so fucking good on my skin."

"Have you ever tried walking on hot coals? There's supposed to be a way to do it where you don't burn the soles of your feet. "

"That sounds like hippie bullshit."

"I saw it on the Montel Williams show so it must be true."

The bonfire devoured the chairs quickly. Kim and Trevor watched it burn for as long as it was interesting. An awkward pause descended on the moment, like a weighted blanket on Trevor's chest. Was this his opportunity to make a move, to sweep Kim off her feet and away from this terrible party? What was he supposed to say? He never seemed to find the right words.

"So..." he started.

"So..." she echoed.

"My place is right around the corner. How about we cruise over there and see if we can start our own fire?"

"I was kind of supposed to meet friends at the Righteous Room for last call."

"Maybe I can join."

"It might be awkward. It's my ex-boyfriend's birthday thing. There's no bad blood and we still have a lot of mutual friends."

"I understand," said Trevor. "I guess."

"I'll see you around?" she asked. "Maybe we'll meet at some other party. If you're as charming then as you have been tonight, maybe I'll let you try out those legendary oral skills out on me. Until then, I'm out of here."

Trevor kissed her on the cheek. He watched her round the corner, then collapsed into the un-mowed grass. Another wasted opportunity. Another night alone. Another instance of getting his hopes up only to be crushed. Was Kim even attracted to him, or was she just playing with his emotions? He should've seen this coming. Why did he allow himself to be manipulated by any attractive female? It was another failure in a lifelong series of failures.

Disappointment plagued him, hung on him like a stink, infected others around him. He was a disappointment to his family for smoking weed and dropping out of college. He was a disappointment to his ex-girlfriend Stacey for refusing to take their relationship seriously. He was a disappointment to all the other ex-girlfriends that preceded Stacey. He was a disappointment to himself. For being so goddamn vulnerable. For hoping that tonight would be different than every other night. For believing that tonight was his shining moment, when he'd win over the pretty girl and ride off hand-in-hand into a technicolour sunset.

Trevor's delicate psyche was shaken. He realised, for the first time, that he was pissing away the prime of his life chasing the unattainable.

Trevor thought he was hot shit— but he was nothing but a cold turd.

HOW TO EAT A CARRIE MANGO

Arlo Einstein was the island's longest serving and most elusive politician. He hadn't talked to the press in decades. He thumped hard on the bible and voters in his district loved him, especially the poor and uneducated.

Einstein was in the news, again, for using homophobic slurs on the People's Assembly floor. Same-sex marriage legislation was up for debate, and Arlo Einstein was the braying mouthpiece of the opposition.

"God created Adam and Eve," he bellowed from the gilded lectern. "Not Adam and Steve!"

Cosmo Archer watched Einstein's speech via video link. The entire Channel Two newsroom gathered around the monitor. The story had huge implications for Grand Calabash. As it stood, it was the last marriage equality holdout in the commonwealth. If the People's Assembly failed to legalise same-sex marriage, the tiny island nation would face sanctions from the crown.

"Something's off about this guy," said Cosmo. "The way he's leaning in to the homophobic hate speech. It's super tone-deaf."

"The poorest people get hit hardest by sanctions, yet they're the ones who elect politicians like Einstein who've been running this country into the dirt," said news director Samantha Tulemon.

"This place is so backwards," said producer Nigel Doggins. "They call it 'the island time forgot' for a reason."

"It's always, 'if we let a man marry a man, what happens next?'" said Samantha. "The argument is that people will want to marry dogs and horses. It's a slippery slope into bestiality.'"

"But the thing is, nobody's out there fucking horses," said Nigel. "It's so predictable how this island retreats into a crabs-in-a bucket mentality. All the government has to do is let people who love each other get married and the threat of sanctions disappear."

"Did you hear that? Einstein just called homosexuality the world's most decadent sin."

"What strange terminology," said Cosmo. "Does that seem like a red flag to anyone else?"

Einstein's rant continued. By the end he was full-throat shouting. "We must fight these deviants, the Johnny-come-latelies who say our island ways are not good enough, that God's word is not good enough. We must fight to preserve our Christian way of life!"

Nigel slid forward in his chair. "Are you suggesting Einstein's living in the closet?"

Samantha raised an eyebrow.

Cosmo chose his words carefully. "The sad thing is, I don't think he even realises it."

"I see what you mean."

"There's no way he's actually gay," said Samantha. "Believe me, Grand Calabash is too small of an island to keep a bombshell like that secret."

"It's always the ones who protest the loudest. Makes you wonder."

"His sexuality is unimportant in the grand scheme of things," said Cosmo. "If he succeeds and blocks the marriage equality bill, Grand Calabash will be the laughing stock of the free world."

Samantha Tulemon assigned Cosmo to chase the Arlo Einstein story. He was a notoriously slippery character, but Cosmo had been softening him up for months. Einstein's only interest outside of fighting the gay agenda was agriculture, specifically mango farming. Cosmo had an in. He and his wife had spent the weekend canning a massive a batch of mango chutney. It was delicious.

Cosmo parked at the edge of the Einstein compound. He left the camera equipment in the car and walked up a short path towards the house. He decided to show up unannounced to present a jar of homemade chutney.

The timing was excellent. Arlo Einstein was in the garage, fussing with his luxury riding lawnmower.

"I thought important lawmakers had landscapers," said Cosmo.

"I do have landscapers," said Arlo. "I just like to drive this little tractor around. It puts me in touch with this beautiful world the lord has made."

Einstein always tried to distract him by dragging him into the existence of God debate. Cosmo was determined not to bite. He maintained a neutral facade as he presented the jar of chutney.

"My wife and I have a Julie mango tree in our backyard. She's been generous this year."

"Julie is a good mango," said Einstein. "But a Carrie mango is truly a life-changing experience. Have you ever tried one?"

Arlo insisted on a tour of the compound, which included the mango orchard, some pasture lands, and sweeping views of Turtle Skull Bay. How could a public servant amass such a fortune? It was a million dollar view. Cosmo climbed on the back of the lawnmower and they rode in tandem, like two cowboys on the same horse.

"Hold on so you don't get thrown off," said Einstein. "Put your arms around my waist."

Cosmo became extremely uncomfortable. Man stacked on man, pressed together like two all-beef patties in a homoerotic double cheeseburger, lurching awkwardly over difficult terrain on a riding lawnmower. Cosmo wrapped his arms around Einstein in a subordinate pose, clinging to the island's most notorious peddler of homophobic hate speech. Was this some sort of sick and twisted foreplay or was Einstein just rattling his cage?

Conversation wasn't easy. Einstein reverted to bible talk whenever he was confronted by anything outside his narrow worldview. Cosmo tried to remain calm, but was distracted by the terrifying idea that vibrations from the lawnmower might stimulate an unwanted erection, something Einstein would certainly feel scraping his kidneys. An involuntary response like that would send the wrong message, taking an already weird encounter to a place he'd rather avoid.

Was this journalism or had it morphed into something else?

Einstein's position was already on the record. Would it advance the story to ask him to clarify his remarks? It was clear that hate speech was hate speech. What was Cosmo doing here, riding around on the back of a politician's lawnmower? More importantly what were Einstein's intentions? This was literally his turf. He was in total control. Cosmo operated close to the edge but a potentially dangerous situation was unfolding. A dialogue about boundaries and consent felt necessary, not the standard operating procedure for a news interview.

Cosmo persisted beyond his doubts. Arlo Einstein was often dismissed as dwelling on the lunatic fringe but was a complex individual if you could look past the demagoguery. Cosmo regarded him as a deplorable but fascinating character, a walking contradiction. Imagine the self-hatred and inner turmoil brewing in Einstein's psyche after a lifetime of suppressing his sexuality.

The Carrie mango tree towered over an open field. Arlo Einstein had a long wooden pole with a basket at the end. He reached up into the tree and collected two ripe mangoes. They were the size of ostrich eggs, with bright yellow skin and red blush on the fatter end.

"A Carrie mango has a thick skin," said Einstein, fondling the mango suggestively with his long, delicate fingers. "We called them juice box mangoes as kids growing up on Grand Calabash because you don't eat them, you drink them."

Cosmo was uncomfortable, but intrigued.

Einstein continued the demonstration. "Squeeze the mango all over until it's sticky. The objective is to release all the juices from inside the soft pulp. Don't be afraid to massage the mango to get the to juice come out."

The way Einstein manipulated his mango bordered on obscenity. The fruit had surrendered its egg-like shape and now resembled a long, distended tube engorged with juice.

"Make a hole at the tip for the juice to come out," he said, unfolding his pocketknife. "Then suck from the fat end of the mango."

Einstein put his mouth around the tip and sucked. He stroked with both hands along its sides. Mango juice trickled in rivulets from the stretched corners of his mouth. How far was this act going to go?

"Looks like you can't handle the girth," said Cosmo, unable to resist a joke.

Maybe it was the wrong move. Would this leave Cosmo's journalistic intentions and cishet masculinity open for misinterpretation? It was so confusing. Was Einstein coming onto him, or had the tables been turned? Was he the one making a pass? Had he walked into a bizarre reverse honeytrap?

Arlo Einstein jerked his mango dry. It hung there in his sticky hands like a wrung-out, depleted cock. Cosmo wished he could un-see the image of Einstein's face slick with mango juice, but it implanted itself onto his cerebral cortex, a new addition to his sprawling warehouses of accumulated trauma.

"Nothing satisfies like a Carrie mango," he said, wiping his mouth with his shirtsleeve. "Now let me watch you eat one."

BITTER BETTY

I usually shop at Jacky White's Market because it's convenient. I use the rooftop carpark, pop down for my essentials, and I'm on my way in a jiffy.

It's not posh like Sainsbury's or M&S, but it has everything I need. Some of the clientele seem a bit sketchy, but that's part of the charm of going into the city centre. Anything can happen at Jacky White's Market.

So when I needed fresh tuna steaks for a mid-week family dinner, I headed straight to Jacky White's Market. I'd never been to the fishmonger's stall before and thought, why not give it a try instead of driving all the way to Fish Quay?

What a mistake.

There was no queue so I walked right up. Off to a great start, until I saw the cheerless woman in a hairnet sitting at the counter, filing her overgrown fingernails. I didn't see a name tag, so I'll call her Bitter Betty.

Bitter Betty was so engrossed with filing her claws I had to fake a cough to get her attention.

"What do you want," she sneered.

I didn't let her attitude upset me at first. Maybe she was having a bad day. I turned on the charm, hoping to cheer her up with my infectious positivity.

"I'm having a great day, in case you were wondering," I said, with jazz hands.

My energy was clearly too much for her. She folded her arms across her chest and scowled. I dropped the jazz hands.

"Your choice. Order some fish, or fuck off."

I was surprised when she cursed at me, but you have to give people the benefit of the doubt. You can never tell what someone might be going through. Her bitter exterior might be a well-cloaked cry for compassion.

I smiled even wider. "I'm looking for some tuna steak actually, half a kilo."

"We don't use the metric system here."

"It's just over a pound."

"Brexit is law of the land, and the EU can shove their bloody metric system," she said, pointing to signs taped on the till. "See what it says here? Customers must place orders in imperial units."

"'I'll take one pound of tuna steak, then" I said. "A little over is fine."

"We don't got any tuna steak."

"You mean, you ran out?"

"No, we didn't run out," she narrowed her eyes. "We don't stock tuna. There's no tuna today or tomorrow or any other day. We don't stock tuna."

"Is that because of Brexit?"

"How would I know if it's because of Brexit?" she snapped. "You're really getting on my tits now. Either buy something or fuck off so I can finish my manicure."

I tried to keep my cool, but Bitter Betty was testing my patience.

"I'm looking for something not too fishy I can partner with sautéed asparagus tips and seasonal roast vegetables for a family dinner."

"Sounds like a bunch of hoity-toity Chef Gordon Ramsay bollocks," she sneered. "We've got mackerel, cod, pollock, arctic char, and sea bream."

I peered through the glass into the display. Whole fish arranged in rows on beds of crushed ice in the display case. The individual fish wore expressions ranging from sadness to surprise. Their glassy lifeless eyes pleaded to me from behind the glass to get my fish elsewhere.

"I don't like the look of these," I said. "Why are they so slimy?"

"It's just a little mucous."

"Oh."

"Mucous is natural."

"So is breast milk but I wouldn't want to pour it over my breakfast cereal."

"If you don't like the fish, we got crabs, prawns, and scallops too."

I could no longer maintain my patina of kindness. Bitter Betty was being a cunt because she enjoyed it. It was time to stop being nice.

"Two minutes ago you were filing those talons of yours," I said, gesturing to the bowls of shellfish in the display case. "Look at those oysters now, they're completely covered in fingernail dust."

She wasn't used to customers asserting themselves. Bitter Betty dropped off the stool and paced behind the counter in a huff. I'd touched a nerve.

"Those are Oysters Rockefeller. That's grated parmesan, not fingernail dust," she said, sending droplets of spittle flying with each syllable. "If you're not gonna buy anything, then fuck off so I can help other customers. This business will not accommodate time-wasters."

I contemplated escalating this battle of wills but decided it wasn't worth it. There were a hundred other places where I could get tuna steaks.

"Enjoy your manicure," I said, as I pushed out a fart and walked away.

I hope it fucking stank.

SHOULD'VE LISTENED TO AGNES

Turk Blanchard should've listened to Agnes. She warned him several times to steer clear of that Curtis Maywell. If he listened to his dear sweet wife, he never would've shot the shit with that son-of-a-bitch in the lawnmower aisle at Blake's Hardware. If he listened to Agnes he never would've followed Curtis Maywell to the Town Pump Tavern for a drink at eleven in the morning, where 'just one beer' turned into several, followed by boilermakers and Jägerbombs. If he listened to Agnes, Turk Blanchard never would've found himself navigating this prickly moral quandary.

All things considered, he was lucky the day was young. Too early yet for Sheriff's deputies to be scouring the roads for drunk drivers. He stumbled out of the Town Pump Tavern, located his Chevrolet Silverado, and hit the highway, keenly aware there'd be hell to pay if he wasn't around when Agnes got home. Turk's driving was predictably subpar, but traffic was light, especially when he reached the countryside. As the house came into sight from the Toxaway Creek bridge he was relieved to see the empty driveway.

The booze hit Turk like a bulldozer once he stepped onto the front porch. He fumbled with his keys, unable to find the right one. Then, from out of nowhere, he was overcome with an urge to piss. He unzipped and aimed his stream at his wife's hydrangea bushes. Agnes obsessed over these hydrangeas, going on and on about soil acidity levels and how maintaining pH levels brings out the true colours of the blossoms. Turk soaked them from stem to roots with his extra foamy beer piss.

Once inside, Turk went straight for the kitchen. There was a note on the fridge from Agnes, reminding him she was playing bridge with the ladies that night and would be home later than usual. Turk grabbed a jar of peanut butter and a spoon and headed for the back garden to sleep off his day-drunk in his favourite lounge chair. He stared through the trees at the twinkling sun, spooning peanut butter from the jar and cursing that no-good Curtis Maywell. The last thing Turk remembered before the sharp, shooting pain was an overwhelming thirst for revenge.

Getting stung was his own damn fault. He'd been asking for it, after all. Before he passed out in the lounge chair, Turk stripped to his boxer shorts and polished off the entire jar of peanut butter. In his drunken state, it had smeared all over his hands and face. He must've scratched himself when dozing off, and in doing so, transferred peanut butter to his coin purse. This piqued the interest of a curious bumblebee. The bumblebee startled when Turk changed position and plunged its stinger deep into his delicate sack.

Turk leaped from his lounge chair, howling and clutching his gonads. The bumblebee was attached to his ball-bag by its stinger, alive and writhing. Immediately he began to swell. By then Turk had sobered up enough to realise he needed to remove the stinger before the swelling got any worse. He gripped the bumblebee between his thumb and nail of his forefinger and gently worked it out, like a fishhook from the mouth of a bluegill bass. He flicked away the bumblebee corpse in disgust.

Turk's scrotum swelled up like a cantaloupe. He bowed his legs to accommodate it and waddled into the house to find the phone book. He winced in pain as he thumbed through the Yellow Pages, wondering what type of doctor was best suited to handle this particular ailment. Discretion was of utmost importance, as Turk was keen to keep the matter private. Not even his sweet Agnes needed to know about this. One name stood out, board-certified urologist Dr. Geronimo Balzac, whose Yellow Pages advert promised new patients a free telephone consultation.

Turk adjusted himself gingerly and dialled Dr. Balzac's number. After several rings, a deadpan voice put him on hold. The music was three generations out of date.

Elevator music, thought Turk as he glanced at his swollen yam-bag, waiting for the good doctor.

"Dr. Balzac here, what can I help you with?"

"Hypothetical question for you, Doc," started Turk. "Let's say an individual was suffering from a bee sting on his undercarriage, and let's say there was an alarming amount of swelling associated with the incident. How exactly would you advise someone to treat this sort of hypothetical scenario?"

"It depends," replied Dr. Balzac. "Sounds like a relatively low-probability scenario. I'd have to know more about the hypothetical victim. Can I get your name, sir?"

"I don't see how my name is germane to this consultation."

The line went silent. Turk thought he'd been put on hold, but he listened closer and heard Dr. Balzac mumbling faintly, as if he'd cupped his hand over the receiver to address someone in the room. Turk couldn't make out what he was saying, but it sounded like the other person was laughing.

"Still there Doc?"

"As long as this phone consultation doesn't veer from the hypothetical, there's no need to know names. Go ahead and describe what symptoms our hypothetical victim is suffering."

"Swelling. Redness. It itches real bad, like when you get a sunburn."

"Hypothetically, of course."

"Yes, of course. There's also some very severe hypothetical throbbing, with searing hypothetical waves of heat pulsating from the epicentre of the sting."

"Ground zero."

"The victim has removed the stinger, and dabbed the wound with a makeshift antiseptic to ensure it retained hypothetical cleanliness."

"Are you referring to whiskey?"

"Very perceptive, Doc."

"Sounds like you're in quite a pickle."

"A very hypothetical pickle."

Dr. Balzac paused. Turk was in agony, hoping Agnes still had that tube of aloe-vera sunburn gel she carried along when they went tubing on Toxaway Creek.

"My professional advice to someone suffering a scrotal sting…"

"Hypothetical scrotal sting."

"I would send our hypothetical victim to the freezer for some frozen peas or other vegetables to apply to the affected area. The cold will reduce the swelling."

"That's genius, I never would've thought."

"Hypothetically," said Dr. Balzac. "But seriously, if you've been stung on your down-below, you need to come to my office so I can give you an antihistamine injection. That's unless you're okay with the prospect of a ruptured scrotal wall, which I don't have to tell you would be a living nightmare."

"Let's say our hypothetical victim is too drunk to drive, Doc, any chance you're available for a house call?"

Dr. Balzac let out a long sigh. "I suppose that could be arranged."

Turk gave his address, hung up the phone, and rummaged for some frozen peas. The freezer was cluttered with pre-prepared lasagnas, which could be quickly baked in the event of unannounced visitors. Grandma Blanchard used to do the same thing. Agnes was a lot like her— a resourceful, no-nonsense woman who didn't waste time mollycoddling the slow and weak. Was that a strength or a flaw? Turk wasn't sure how he felt about that.

Turk found the frozen peas under a slab of beef brisket, wrapped them in a dish towel, and applied the makeshift cold compress to his swollen undercarriage, hoping Dr. Balzac's shot could stop the swelling before Agnes found out. If his dear sweet wife found out, he would be in deep shit.

"Come on in," Turk hollered from the kitchen table when the doorbell rang. Dr. Balzac entered the room with a leather medical bag in his hand and a stethoscope around his neck. He pulled up a chair and sat knee-to-knee with Turk.

"Before I look at the goods, are you going to tell me your name?" he said as he pulled on a blue latex glove. "It doesn't seem fair for me to be poking around in your intimate areas without knowing some details."

"Curtis Maywell," lied Turk.

"Alright Curtis, let's see this bee sting."

Turk eased himself off his frozen peas and pulled his boxers down around his ankles. Dr. Balzac, the consummate professional, leaned in for a closer look. His scrotum was bright red and resembled a set of conjoined pomegranates. He traced his gloved hand along the pus-ringed crater where the bumblebee plunged its stinger, causing Turk to reflexively jerk away.

"Does it hurt when I do that?"

"What do you think?" snapped Turk. "The whole thing hurts, but it's especially bad where you're touching now."

Dr. Balzac held a flashlight to the wound. Turk's yam-bag glowed like a salt lamp. The scrotal skin was stretched thin, almost to its breaking point. The flashlight's warm glow revealed a dizzying network of capillaries spiderwebbing beneath the skin.

"You're lucky you called when you did, Curtis," said Dr. Balzac, rummaging through his bag for a vial of medication. "Another hour and you'd be dealing with scrotal rupture, which would require multiple surgeries to repair."

Dr. Balzac produced a syringe and filled it with clear white liquid.

"Have you ever had a severe reaction to insect stings?"

"I got stung between the fingers at a swim meet when I was twelve," explained Turk. "The starting gun went off, I leapt off the blocks, and the bee got me before I hit the water. I ended up swimming the race of a lifetime because my hand swelled up twice its size. I used it like a kayak paddle and won a blue ribbon."

"Did you require medical attention?"

"My Aunt Carol took me to the hospital and they gave me a shot for the swelling. I missed the rest of the meet and because of that, my team lost the relay, and because of that we didn't qualify for State. I went from hero to zero that day."

"What a shame," Dr. Balzac shook his head. He was ready to administer the shot. "This is your basic antihistamine/anti-inflammatory cocktail. They teach this on the first day of medical school. It does the trick but it'll feel like a donkey's kick. Ready?"

Turk steeled himself for the needle, clenching his body. Dr. Balzac made the injection into the fatty tissue at the base of the pubic bone. It felt like hot lightning going in, then icy cool as the medicine entered his blood stream.

"How about something for the pain?"

"If you're thinking opiates, that's a hard no," said Dr. Balzac. "I can write you a prescription for Ibuprofen but you probably have that in your cabinets already."

"How about codeine? Quaaludes? Valium?"

"No can do, like I said…"

"I expect you'll be sending a bill for this home visit," Turk interrupted, jerking upright in his chair and startling Dr. Balzac. His eyes widened as he spoke. "You see, if I had some pills to sell, it would help me afford to pay for services you've so kindly rendered. Hell, we could make an arrangement for regular therapy, at a very attractive rate, in exchange for your cooperation."

"Are you asking me to collude with you on a drug-dealing operation?"

"Sounds harsh when you put it that way, Doc. I prefer to call it a profit-sharing venture between two enterprising individuals."

"If you can't afford to pay for the visit I won't charge you, Curtis."

The refrigerator hummed in the ensuing silence, broken when Dr. Balzac abruptly pushed back his chair. The friction on the linoleum created a loud farting noise that broke the growing tension and caused both men to laugh like immature teenagers.

"I'll pretend you never asked that question," he said as he zipped his medical bag. "The swelling should ease up in an hour or two. Keep the frozen peas on there until then. Call me if it gets any worse."

"Thanks Doc. I appreciate your discretion."

Turk found his feet and fished a beer out of the fridge. The frozen peas dulled the throbbing, and whatever Dr. Balzac injected seemed to be working. The conjoined pomegranates had deflated somewhat. Wrinkles had reappeared on his scrotal sac, but the redness remained. He sipped at the beer and pondered his next move. Under no circumstances could he allow Agnes to initiate any sort of hanky-panky. One look at his beleaguered ball-bag and she'd start asking uncomfortable questions.

The frozen peas warmed under his body weight. Turk adjusted himself, flipping the bag over to expose the cold side and fitting them to the contours of his anatomy. He was running out of time to enjoy the soothing sensation. Agnes would be home within the hour and he couldn't be seen sitting on a bag of frozen peas.

Turk drained his beer and slammed the empty can on the table. He went to the fridge for another and noticed a gallon jug of cheap pink wine called Pink Panther. The stuff curdled his stomach but it was Agnes' beverage of choice. If he could get her drunk she wouldn't ask any uncomfortable questions.

Turk's plan was genius. Dinner would be ready when Agnes got home. He'd give her a big glass of Pink Panther. He'd keep that glass full while he encouraged her to dish the latest gossip from the bridge club. Eventually she'd get tipsy and tire herself out without discovering the bee sting on his undercarriage, and more importantly, the fact that he'd been out day-drinking with that no-good Curtis Maywell. Agnes could absolutely not know about that, not before he did what had to be done.

Turk was standing over the stove when Agnes got home. She came through the kitchen like a whirlwind, flinging her purse onto the table and dumping her work lanyard and car keys like on the countertop like unwanted trash.

"You're making dinner... for me?"

"You deserve it, baby," smiled Turk. "Applewood-smoked pork chops for my sweetheart. Slip into something a little more comfortable and it'll be ready to eat when you come back."

Turk drained the grease from the pork chops. He placed them on the table next to a bowl of instant mashed potatoes and the same frozen peas that had, until very recently, provided a valuable therapeutic service. Steam rose from the bowl, and the peas gave no indication they had been pressed against Turk's yam-bag. He cracked a fresh beer for himself and poured a large glass of Pink Panther for Agnes.

"I'm so impressed," she said when she saw the spread.

"I'm no Michelin-star chef, but I gave it my best shot," said Turk, raising his beer. "Cheers baby— now tell me all about your day."

With that, Agnes was off to the races. Apparently there'd been major shakeups in the socio-political hierarchy of the bridge club. Turk followed the storylines as best he could, but there were too many characters involved. He nodded his head at appropriate times and reacted with outrage when he sensed it was called for. He ate slowly, methodically slicing his pork chop into wafer thin pieces and submerging each bite in Worcestershire sauce before bringing the fork his mouth. Each time Agnes took a sip of Pink Panther he nonchalantly topped up her glass.

"I just don't see why Bernadette struggles so hard just to keep up appearances," she said, her voice growing louder. "Everyone knows her husband lost his job, and it's no secret why his dumb ass got fired."

"Bernadette's the one with the bad perm and big round glasses?"

"She does have a bad perm, but you're thinking of Theresa, who by the way is also a huge bitch who needs to mind her damn manners."

Agnes was practically shouting now, a sure sign the Pink Panther was kicking in. She was a loud talker when she was on the wine.

"Bernadette's always selling mail-order cosmetics and wearing her skirts too short. I swear, she wants everybody to see her breakfast. I think you know her husband Samuel."

"Samuel Pickford?" Turk scratched his head. "The guy who got caught on CCTV taking a piss into his boss' coffee cup at the car dealership?"

"So, Bernadette shows up with an armload of Krispy Kreme doughnuts, like she's doing us a favour," she continued, "Then Lucille jumps in like, 'Bernadette, you shouldn't have, seriously, save your pennies because we all know Samuel's unemployment runs out soon,' just saying out loud what everyone else is thinking."

Turk kept Agnes talking. They migrated to the living room sofa after dinner and he brought the Pink Panther along, topping her up continuously until she was faintly snoring. He tiptoed back to the kitchen where he took a seat at the table with pen and paper. Better keep it short and sweet, he thought.

"Dear Agnes," he wrote. "I was out drinking with Curtis Mayfield today and he told me what happened between the two of you last summer when I was out of town for my Grandaddy's funeral. I know Curtis is a no-good son-of-a-bitch, and expect that bastard to act like a bastard. But I didn't expect you to be the one to do me dirty. In light of this unexpected betrayal I have no choice but to leave this marriage. I used to think we were soul mates but I guess I was wrong."

Turk folded the note, put it on the counter by her keys, and took a long last look around the house they shared. It was full of memories, mostly good ones. He should've listened to Agnes and stayed away from that no-good Curtis Mayfield. If he only would've listened to his dear sweet Agnes, everything could've stayed the same. If he would've stayed away from that son-of-a-bitch he never would've learned the hard truth.

It's been said that the truth will set you free. But what was freedom if you didn't have someone special to share it with? Freedom was a crock of shit. Freedom could suck a big fat dick. Fuck freedom. Nothing mattered anymore. Not even freedom.

Turk Blanchard took a deep breath before stepping into the night, not bothering to collect his belongings, not knowing where to go next. From now on, he would walk alone.

THE SHOW MUST GO ON

Cosmo Ardmore whistled out loud as he prepared graphics for his Out Of This World™ forecast in the NewsChannel 9 WeatherPlex. Lingering high pressure meant clear skies and warm afternoons, ideal weather for backyard badminton and barbecues, the kind of forecast his viewers loved to see. He dragged a row of smiling sunglasses-wearing sunshines into the seven day forecast to emphasise the point.

A spectacular crash interrupted his songbird imitation, the sound of in-studio guests running amok in the green room. He pressed CNTRL-S to save his work and headed to investigate.

A troupe of juggling acrobats were recovering after toppling their pyramid stunt. They were the first of three special guests on that morning's edition of Have A Nice Day, the highest rated morning news programme in the metropolitan Tri-Cities area.

"Everything okay in here?"

A tall skinny acrobat brushed dust from his pants-leg. "The coffee's a little weak, otherwise we're all good."

Cosmo flashed his larger-than-life smile, the one featured on dozens of gleaming NewsChannel 9 billboards stationed alongside all the major thoroughfares in the metropolitan Tri-Cities area.

"Let's save that energy for the show, my friends. The viewers absolutely go bananas when an act like yours falls apart."

"Don't worry about our act," said a short round acrobat. "You should be worried about the guy with the tigers."

A man in zookeeper khakis entered the room, leading a pair of juvenile tigers. The acrobat had a point, animal acts were inherently unpredictable. That's why they made such great television, because the viewers, the hosts, and studio crew had no idea what would happen.

"I'm Bill Habersham, the Big Cat Man," he said, extending his hand for a shake. "The one on the left is Tasha, and the other one is Sasha. They were rescued from a Mexican circus, both of them sweet girls, very intelligent and very well trained."

"Great to meet you, Bill," said Cosmo, still pumping away on the handshake. "Help yourselves to a cup of coffee and I'll let the producers know you're here."

Cosmo ducked into the hallway, shut the green room door behind him, and headed towards the control room. A circus-like atmosphere wasn't out of the ordinary at the NewsChannel 9 studios. Have A Nice Day's ratings success was due in large part to its unpredictability. In absence of a winning formula, the producers just took spaghetti and flung it at the wall. More often than not, it stuck.

Cosmo poked his head into the control room, where a frantic production staff was making last-minute adjustments to the rundown. Before he could spit out a hello he was peppered with questions from Janette O'Keefe, the show's highly-strung executive producer.

"Are you okay with two-thirty for your first weather hit?"

"Affirmative."

"Did you see I put you in for a ten second tease at the end of the A-block?"

"Wouldn't miss it for the world."

"Did you know you're wearing the same tie you had on yesterday?"

"Negative."

"Do me a favour and change it," she said. "We don't need another phone call from Businessman's Emporium. They pay us shitloads of money to sponsor your wardrobe, so keep rocking those fresh new ties. No repeats."

Cosmo loosened his half-Windsor and nodded. Janette's eye for detail was astounding. To him, all neckties looked the same.

"Have you seen the aromatherapy lady?"

"No, but the juggling acrobats and the tiger act are camped out and ready to go."

"That's fantastic," Janette said, pushing him out of the control room. "If you see the aromatherapy lady, send her down to the green room."

Cosmo glanced at his watch. He had five minutes to change his tie, dust himself with on-air makeup, and get in place for the round-robin, Have A Nice Day's rapid-fire opening segment.

He felt a surge of nervous energy, not exactly butterflies, but a heightened sense of internal awareness that preceded a television appearance. No matter how many thousands of times he stood in front of the cameras to ad-lib the weather, he felt a small surge of adrenaline. He made it look easy, with his self-deprecating demeanour and gleaming weatherman grin, but every segment was a tightrope act. A single misstep could send the forecast careening towards a crash and burn. This was a television presenter's worst nightmare, when two seconds floundering for speech felt like ten thousand eternities. What the viewers never realised was that being a weatherman only looked easy because he made it look easy.

"Cosmo Ardmore," bellowed sound engineer Jericho Brown. "Did you know you're wearing the same tie you had on yesterday?"

"Janette told me already."

"I know," he said. "Her royal highness asked me to remind you to change the damn thing before we hit the air. Now, let me get you wired up for sound."

Cosmo threaded the microphone cable through the buttonholes of his shirt while Jericho fastened the transmitter to his belt. The lapel microphone dangled under his chin like a wilted tulip while Cosmo carefully knotted his replacement tie.

"Testing, testing... three, two, one... how's that sound?"

"Clear as bells. Get your earpiece stuffed in and park your ass at the WeatherPlex so they can get you framed up on camera three."

Cosmo took his place in front of the SuperDoppler 9000 radar monitor. Over at the news desk, morning anchors Kip Clifford and Penelope Gonzales shuffled their paper scripts. The unwritten rule in broadcast news was that a male anchor must appear taller than his female co-anchor. Penelope, who was six inches taller than Kip, lowered her chair in deference to traditional gender roles. Across the studio, in the SportsPlex, the glamorous Kristin Ng, a former Miss Tri-Cities runner-up, tugged at the hem of her skirt to keep it from riding up her sculpted thighs.

"Good morning, my lovelies," crackled Janette's voice through the earpiece. "One minute and thirty seconds to the show. I want to see big time energy this morning, so let's give me bright eyes and bushy tails for the round-robin. You can sleep when you're dead."

"Ten seconds," called out the floor director.

Cosmo bounced on the balls of his feet as the countdown commenced. This must be how an astronaut feels before being blasted into space, he thought.

"We're in the open," said Janette through the earpiece, as the familiar strains of the Have A Nice Day anthem blared through the studio loudspeaker. "Standby Kip and Penelope on camera one... mic and cue."

"Good morning, I'm Kip Clifford. An overnight fire in the Tri-Cities leaves three families homeless, we'll show you the everyday household item fire investigators say is responsible for the devastating blaze."

"I'm Penelope Gonzalez. Most of us can agree that cupcakes are delicious, but can they help win the war on childhood cancer? One local teenager thinks so. That inspiring story later."

"A big night in Tri-Cities basketball as the Screaming Condors soar above the competition at Blaart Intercontinental Coliseum. I'm Kristin Ng and I'll have all the highlights."

Cosmo smiled into the lens. In journalism school he was taught to address the camera as if it were a best friend, but to him, it was much more than that. The camera was his source of income, his self-worth, it was his everything.

When the red light finally came on, he launched into his energetic spiel.

"Sunny skies will stick around as a trough of high pressure reigns supreme. I'm Cosmo Ardmore and you won't want to miss my Out Of This World™ forecast."

The round-robin closed with a sweeping two-shot of Kip and Penelope at the news desk, reminding the viewers in unison to "Have a Nice Day" before going to commercial.

"You guys nailed it," said Janette. "Let's keep that energy going."

Cosmo turned down his earpiece volume so he could concentrate on his remaining graphics. Putting them together was easy enough, with hundreds of pre-built templates and animations to choose from. The time-consuming part was ensuring the data fields were populated with accurate, up-to-the-minute information.

Predicting the weather was a crapshoot. Sometimes he got it right, and sometimes he fell on his ass trying. It was the nature of the business. The powerful SuperDoppler 9000 system brought technological advancements to the table, but concocting a forecast was still a guessing game, a divination comparable to reading tarot cards. Cosmo learned from the best, the great Bob McGuinness, a no-nonsense weatherman who used to step outside the studio, wet his index finger with saliva, and hold it to the air to gauge the changing weather. Bob McGuinness never had a SuperDoppler 9000 at his disposal, but he guessed the weather as well as anybody.

Cosmo's earpiece crackled to life. Janette again. "Can we get you in front of camera three? Your weather tease is in exactly one minute."

Cosmo hit CNTRL-S to save his work and took his position at the WeatherPlex desk. The anchors were giving their reaction to a feel-good story about a so-called good samaritan with a metal detector who found a couple's missing engagement ring, returning it just in time for their anniversary.

"What a powerful story," said Kit, in his booming baritone. "The kindness of strangers."

"It's extraordinary. What are the chances?" Penelope said, pivoting to the segue. "Speaking of chances, Cosmo Ardmore joins us in the WeatherPlex, should we expect showers this week?"

"In a word, no, Penelope," Cosmo picked up the toss with his larger-than-life smile. "You'd have a better chance of finding missing jewellery than encountering any measurable precipitation, I'll have more details a little later..."

Janette popped in his ear, frantically. "Tease the acrobats, tease the acrobats."

Cosmo hated when the producers interrupted him when he was live on-air. Unless there was some sort of emergency there was no need for it. Still, he managed to keep his composure, and threw a strong toss to the commercial break.

"...plus, the high-flying acrobats of Tumbling Tumbleweeds will be live in the studio to juggle their way into your hearts, that and so much more to come this morning on Have A Nice Day."

"You're a freakin' rockstar, Coz," said a very relieved Janette in the earpiece. "I know it's last minute, but do you mind reading the intro to the acrobats in studio B?"

Even though it was framed as a question, Cosmo had no free will in the matter. Janette was the show's executive producer and her word was law.

"I can't imagine a bigger career opportunity," he joked.

"That kind of attitude will get you an extra thirty seconds for weather," said Janette. "By the way, there's nothing in the prompter, so you'll have to wing it."

He would've delivered a snappy comeback, but his microphone was already muted. Janette had moved on to other pressing issues, making the most of the two minute commercial break.

The juggling acrobats were ready for action in cavernous studio B, a repurposed aircraft hangar. It was big enough to host a marching band, if necessary, with high ceilings to accommodate trapeze artists and other circus performers. Tumbling Tumbleweeds had plenty of space to do their thing. Cosmo took his place on a yellow X in front of the jib camera's long boom arm. He would give his introduction and the camera rig would swoop over him to a wide shot of the juggling acrobats.

"Break a leg, you guys," said Cosmo. "And please, don't take that literally. The ironclad performance waiver you signed holds NewsChannel 9 and its employees harmless in the event of death, dismemberment, or other serious injury incurred on the premises. I hope you can keep your pyramid together this time."

The tall skinny acrobat pantomimed side-splitting laughter. "Don't worry about us, we can do these stunts drunk and in our sleep."

The short round acrobat stuck out his tongue and raised a middle finger. "We got the best health insurance there is, so mind your own beeswax."

Cosmo rolled his eyes and turned back to the camera. Harmless studio banter, all in good fun, as long as the rude gestures don't make the airwaves.

"Coming to you in thirty seconds," Janette was back in his ear. "Don't stray too far, if an acrobat falls and cracks their skull open, I'm cutting to you on camera four."

He signalled okay with his thumb and forefinger.

"Ten seconds."

Cosmo found himself strapped into the capsule once again, ready to launch. The beauty of these ad-libbed segments was that he had no idea what he was going to say until he said it. When the red light went on, the words tumbled out of him without thought.

"Welcome back to Have A Nice Day, I'm Cosmo Ardmore. We have a real treat for you this morning, please welcome our special guests to the show, the high-flying, electrifying, daredevil acrobats of Tumbling Tumbleweeds."

The acrobats were entertaining, mugging for the cameras as they performed their intricate choreography, juggling various objects, starting out with rings and advancing to bowling pins and flaming torches. The short round acrobat functioned as ringleader, signalling the troupe to change formations and distributing the props.

"Can you believe these guys?" said Janette in his earpiece. "One mistake could burn down the whole studio."

The organ music accelerated as the act neared its climax, the juggling tower. The performers huddled together, forming the base of the human pyramid, then hoisting members into place for a second, then third tier, all to the pulsating beat of the music. The flaming torches were swapped for chainsaws to add an additional element of danger to the grand finale.

"They're wrapping up," she said. "Standby."

The jugglers leaped from the pyramid one-by-one, tossing their chainsaws into the air. They manoeuvred through a series of acrobatic embellishments as they vaulted to the ground, just in time to catch their chainsaws and extend their arms in victorious poses.

"Once again, ladies and gentlemen, the juggling acrobats of Tumbling Tumbleweeds," said Cosmo, gesturing to the smiling performers behind him. "Tickets are still available for tonight's performance at the Blaart Intercontinental Coliseum— it's a show you won't want to miss. Have A Nice Day will be back with more news and entertainment after the break."

Cosmo congratulated the acrobats and headed back to the WeatherPlex to look busy. The true artistry of being a weatherman was giving the impression that you were overwhelmed with work even when you weren't. Dropping the facade meant risking being recruited to assist the production team with any number of random and often unpleasant chores.

"Hey rockstar," said Janette through the earpiece. "I need another favour. Come see me in the control room and I'll fill you in."

Competence was a curse in the newsroom. If an employee showed flashes of it, management would pile on additional responsibilities until that person's spirit was broken and all that remained was the desiccated husk of their former self. Meanwhile, incompetent employees were routinely elevated into managerial positions because they weren't cut out for life in the trenches. It was called falling upward. These people entrenched themselves in brutal fiefdoms within the organisational hierarchy, bludgeoning their underlings with the brute force of their asinine expectations. This phenomenon was the single biggest contributing factor in burnout and high turnover in the TV news business.

Cosmo caught Janette's attention through the control room glass. She held up a finger, indicating she would be with him once she's dealt with whatever crisis was unfolding in there. He knew better than to go in the booth during a show. The control room was the nerve centre of the station, and stress levels often reached radioactive levels.

Janette popped out, clutching her clipboard, as always.

"Is everything okay?"

"Putting out fires, as usual. Nothing three bottles of Pinot Grigio won't fix after the credits roll," she said. "We're having technical issues at the moment, so I was hoping I could count on you to take charge of the rest of today's guest segments."

"Sure thing."

"I've restructured the rundown so the guests go back-to-back in the same segment. That way you'll have time to get back to the WeatherPlex for your big weather hit, which I've had to trim down to two minutes."

"Whatever gets us through the show."

"I owe you a beer."

"Make it a six pack," he said. "I'm on it."

Cosmo hurried to the green room to collect the guests. He had less than ten minutes to get them to studio B for their segments.

"Good morning again," he said cheerily. "Can you please follow me to the studio?"

Bill Habersham and his twin tigers, Tasha and Sasha, were leashed up and ready to go, but the aromatherapy lady, a white-haired woman who looked extremely old, was still arranging her array of scented candles on a velvety pedestal.

"I'm not ready," she protested. "Look at all these candles!"

"You'll have plenty of time to get ready once we're in the studio," said Cosmo. "Does this thing have wheels? I'll help push."

He escorted his guests through the maze of hallways leading to studio B. The aromatherapy lady, who introduced herself as Hazel Maitland, was not a fast walker. This, and the constant stream of production interns stopping Bill Habersham to request selfies with Tasha and Sasha, had Cosmo worried the guests might miss their time slot.

"There will be no selfies until after the segment," said Cosmo, taking control of the situation. Interns always respected the weatherman. "Interns, can you please escort the lovely Miss Hazel down to studio B."

Jericho Brown was already there, wielding lavaliere microphones. "Two minutes."

Cosmo directed the interns to help set up Miss Hazel's aromatherapy candles on the far side of the studio while Jericho wired Bill Habersham for sound.

"One minute," said Janette through the earpiece. "Are the guests ready?"

Cosmo shrugged into the camera. Despite the hours of pre-production planning and preparation, despite the collective due diligence of the assembled team of seasoned professionals, success was never a given in live television. That was the allure of the industry, the adrenaline surging through your system as you charged full steam ahead into the oncoming train wreck.

"Thirty seconds," called out Jericho. "I think we're going to make it."

"I've got ice water in my veins," said Cosmo.

He took his place on the yellow X and beckoned for Bill Habersham to join him with Tasha and Sasha. With no time to brief either guest on what to expect, he felt poised on the cliff's edge, about to step into the great unknown.

"Ten seconds," said Janette in his earpiece. "You got this."

Cosmo pushed all thought from his mind as the seconds ticked down. Better not to overthink things and let his instincts take over. The camera's red light came on and the words spilled out like honey from a jar. He ad-libbed his way through the introduction and turned the programme over to Bill Habersham the Big Cat Man, who ran Tasha and Sasha through a series of increasingly complicated tricks to a medley of Michael Jackson's greatest hits.

"We'll give the tigers another two minutes," she said. "We need you in front of camera five with the aromatherapy lady. One of the interns will give Habersham the wrap signal."

Miss Hazel had constructed a towering ziggurat of aromatherapy candles on her velvet pedestal, but she struggled to light them with her spindly arms. An intern jumped in to offer assistance. The duelling aromas of sandalwood and juniper berry soon filled the studio.

Bill Habersham turned to face the camera. "Tasha and Sasha are big fans of the King of Pop, and for their final trick this morning, they're going to do the moonwalk."

The Big Cat Man blew sharply into his whistle and the tigers stood up on their hind legs. He whistled again and they went into motion, gliding across the shiny studio floor to the throbbing bass line of Billie Jean. It was bizarre and hypnotic in equal measure, a performance engineered to titillate an audience.

"Standby," said Janette.

The interns flashed the wrap cue at Bill Habersham. He summoned Tasha and Sasha to the centre of the studio for an exaggerated final bow, squatting between the two tigers and letting them lick the sides of his face. It was compelling television.

The director cut to camera five, and once again Cosmo was live with the aromatherapy lady. It was her first television appearance and nerves were getting the best of her. She trembled with stage-fright next to the weatherman.

"Our next guest is here to introduce you to the beneficial healing properties of scent," said Cosmo. "Please welcome the one and only Miss Hazel Maitland, known affectionately throughout the metropolitan Tri-Cities area as the aromatherapy lady."

She stared at the camera with blank eyes. Cosmo had seen that look before, the petrified face of a guest paralysed by fear. The old bag was having a panic attack, and it was on him to keep the energy flowing through the segment.

"I have to say," he ad-libbed, killing time. "It's a shame we don't have smell-a-vision technology, because these scented candles are amazingly fragrant. Miss Hazel, how many different scents do we have here?"

She moved her lips feebly but made no sound.

"It seems like way too many to count, to be honest," he said, struggling to keep the one-sided conversation afloat. "And I see that you also have aromatherapy oils?"

Miss Hazel nodded.

Cosmo was just about to toss to commercial break when he detected in his peripheral vision an object streaking towards him at a high rate of speed. One of the tigers had broken away from Bill Habersham. Cosmo braced himself for impact but the animal skirted by, grazing his knees.

Miss Hazel clutched at her side. "Sweet Jesus!"

Cosmo was disoriented. Everything seemed to be happening in slow motion. Another tiger zoomed past, sideswiping the aromatherapy pedestal and sending hundreds of scented candles crashing to the studio floor. Jars of essential oil became molotov cocktails, exploding on impact. Through the chaos he maintained his composure, addressing the camera as if it were his best friend. He opened his mouth and words came out.

"As you can see we are experiencing some technical difficulties," he said. "Anything can happen in a live broadcast, and the Have A Nice Day team are working to get it under control."

Tigers zigzagged across the studio as Cosmo continued ad-libbing. An intern dragged Miss Hazel away from the flames. Bill Habersham and the other interns chased after Tasha and Sasha, trying desperately to get the big cats under control.

"This is great stuff," said Janette in his earpiece. "Keep up the energy!"

"As you can see, the flames are spreading rather quickly," said Cosmo, flashing his larger-than-life smile at the camera's lens. "Keep in mind that we here at NewsChannel 9 plan for all contingencies, so you can feel secure in knowing the studio curtains have been fully treated with flame retardant chemicals. There's no need to panic, as the situation is under control."

"Don't quit on me now," said Janette. "Toss to commercial."

The studio filled with smoke. Cosmo felt the searing heat from all directions. He was surrounded on all sides by a ring of fire. If ever there was a time for him to shine, this was it. His legacy was at stake. A true professional presses on through adversity because the show must go on. He focused the entire energy of his being on that beacon before him, the camera's red light, and opened his mouth to speak.

"Coming up after the break," he said, fighting the overpowering urge to choke on the thickening smoke. "More news and entertainment on Have A Nice Day."

MR. PINK

Ariel was Owen's girlfriend and Owen was Dexter's boss. They were at the bar together, after closing time, when Ariel mentioned she was moving into a new flat and needed an extra set of hands.

"It's not much stuff really." Ariel stirred the ice cube remnants in her vodka tonic. "A few boxes, a love seat, some other bits and bobs."

"You're free Saturday morning?" said Owen.

Dexter couldn't say no. That's how he found himself at the bottom of the staircase, straining to brace a giant oak armoire with his body. Ariel's brother Keith handled the top end, taking his sweet time.

"I need to adjust my grip," whined Keith. "My delicate hands are slipping."

"Hurry up, this thing is heavy."

"Try carrying it backwards."

"Let's just get it up the stairs. I smell McDonald's."

Once inside, Ariel distributed Egg McMuffins. Dexter scraped a small triangle of stuck-on melted cheese from the wrapper and opened the sandwich for inspection. When he determined it was unadulterated by pubic hair or other contaminants, he took a bite.

"They crack the egg into a cookie cutter on the griddle, so they come out in perfect McMuffin-sized circles," said Keith.

"No way!" squealed Ariel. "I've always wondered how they got the Egg McMuffins into perfect circles."

"I worked at Mickey D's in high school. Learned all the tricks."

Keith was getting on Dexter's nerves.

"Then why present your insider Egg McMuffin knowledge like it's some kind of state secret? Everybody knows the cookie cutter trick."

"Working at McDonald's is more complicated than it looks. It takes a lot of effort to get it right."

Dexter changed the subject, addressing Ariel. "Are we almost done?"

"You can't leave yet. There's still so much to do," she protested. "We need to put everything where it belongs. Owen should be here any minute with my dad."

"Classic Owen, showing up to help after the worst part's finished," said Keith. "Honestly, I don't know why you stay with that guy, he's at least twenty years older than you. He's old enough to be your dad."

"My dad is your dad too. Besides, I happen to like older men," said Ariel. "Now shut up, they're here."

Two sets of footsteps tromped noisily up the stairs. Dexter could hear Owen and Ariel's dad laughing about something.

"Nice place," said Owen. "Any Egg McMuffins left?"

"Egg McMuffins are off-limits until you've done some manual labour," said Ariel.

Owen ignored her and took an Egg McMuffin. There were handshakes all around as Ariel introduced everybody. Keith was right, Owen was old enough to be her father. Ariel's dad had more grey hair but they looked similar, two middle age white guys who might play racquetball together after work.

"Marian just called," said Owen. "She and Brian are running late."

"I wish you wouldn't call my Mom by her first name around me," said Ariel. "It's kind of creepy."

"Sorry baby-cakes, force of habit. We went to high school together," said Owen.

Dexter, Roger, and Keith worked while Owen sat and played games on his phone. The bed was an elaborate four-poster with colour coded nuts and bolts. Dexter and Roger held the massive headboard upright while Keith threaded the hardware and barked out commands.

"Dexter, raise your corner post two inches, hold it there, that's perfect."

Ariel's Mom and her fiancé Brian arrived just as Dexter, Roger, and Keith finished the bed frame. Ariel's Mom cheerily held up a large McDonald's bag.

"Anyone hungry?"

"Mom, I've already fed the crew."

"The more McMuffins the merrier."

Owen stopped playing on his phone long enough to grab another McMuffin.

"Thanks for these, Marian," he said. "Candy Crush always makes me super hungry."

Dexter unwrapped and inspected another McMuffin. There were a million places he'd rather be than Ariel's flat, suffocating in this bizarre family dynamic. Strange lines of tension pulled in competing directions.

After Egg McMuffins it was time to put the mattress and box spring in place. Owen returned to Candy Crush and let everyone else do the work. They eased the queen-size box spring into place on the rails of the frame. The memory foam mattress was next. It was marshmallowy soft and rolled up like a burrito. With mammoth effort they managed to hoist it onto the bed.

Once in place, Keith cut the strips of tape that held it together. The mattress unfurled like a toy snake leaping from a prank tin of peanuts, launching a monstrous pink dildo into the air. The dildo landed with a thump on the hardwood floor and rolled across the bedroom, coming to a stop in front of Ariel's dad.

There was a long, awkward silence. Dexter glanced back and forth between the dildo and the horrified faces of Ariel's mother and father. No one wanted to touch it for self-explanatory reasons.

"Ariel, can you come here for a second?" said Marian.

"Sure, what's up?"

Ariel entered the silent room and was confronted with the scene. Her mother nodded wordlessly at the massive dildo while everyone else pretended they were somewhere else.

"Oh, there you are, Mr. Pink," said Ariel. She scooped it up and put it in a drawer. "I've been looking everywhere for you."

Dexter wanted to laugh but was voiceless, like he was in a nightmare and unable to scream. All these fathers and daughters and dildos, mothers and brothers and dildos, sisters and boyfriends and dildos, exes and fiancees and dildos. Bosses and girlfriends and dildos. Candy Crush and Egg McMuffins and dildos. Where did he fit into this bizarre cast of characters? He was just a guy who inadvertently got roped into helping move furniture.

Ariel's voice drifted in from the living room.

"There's more Egg McMuffins if anyone wants one."

ANOTHER SATISFIED CUSTOMER

Reginald Atwater wasted the early prime of his life as a Sub-Works sandwich artisan in the Omaha suburbs. If he would've realised this back then he would've quit making sandwiches and done something meaningful with his life, like becoming a surf instructor in Costa Rica.

Instead he devoted himself to sandwich artisanship, confident his work ethic and commitment to craft would gain the attention of the higher-ups. He was what they called 'a real team player,' willing to sacrifice his personal plans on short notice to cover when less dedicated Sub-Works sandwich artisans failed to show up for duty. It was only a matter of time, he thought, that he would be rewarded with the promotion to management he so staunchly believed he deserved.

Reginald was already de facto weekend manager, trusted with keys to the safe and alarm codes to the highest-grossing Sub-Works location in the greater Omaha area. At closing time he was responsible for the paperwork, counting cash, collating receipts, bundling it all together in a leather zip pouch for the day-shift manager to deposit at the bank the following day. The way he saw it, he was ready to take up the mantle of a full-fledged Sub-Works manager. Making bank deposits. Processing payroll. Hiring, firing, and employee discipline.

Cornhusker Plaza was an ideal location for a sandwich shop. In addition to the highest-grossing Sub-Works store in the greater Omaha area, it housed a day-old bakery outlet, a gas station that sold trucker speed and porn magazines, a shoe repair store, a flower shop, two competing insurance agents, and Miss Janet's International Academy of Interpretive Dance.

This thriving small business community generated a steady flow of traffic to Sub-Works, but Cornhusker Plaza's anchor tenant was CJ's Poop Deck, a sports-themed bar and grill.

Reginald despised CJ's Poop Deck and everything it stood for. The idea of reasonably-priced bacon double cheeseburgers and triple-smoked hot buffalo wings siphoning revenue from Sub-Works was sickening enough, but CJ's revolving smorgasbord of lowbrow entertainment truly disgusted him. From karaoke tournaments and Foghat cover bands to whipped cream bikini wrestling contests, there was always something happening at CJ's to bring out the drunks. He hated when drunks stumbled into Sub-Works at closing time, when the counters had been cleaned and the vegetables stashed away in the walk-in cooler. Poop Deck drunks were almost invariably indecisive and ill-tempered, reeking of cheap beer and cigarette smoke, demanding a made-to-order Sub-Works sandwich yet lacking the ability to coherently articulate their desired toppings.

•

CJ's Poop Deck did peak business during football season. Like a typical sports bar, CJ's was outfitted with a ridiculous number of big screen televisions, rendering it practically impossible for a Poop Deck patron to miss a single electrifying second of bone-crunching NFL action. It could get pretty rowdy in there. During the game, a bucket of beer was half price. When a touchdown was scored, 25¢ tequila shots flowed and 'The Power of Love' by Huey Lewis and the News blasted from the stereo. This was wholesome middle-American entertainment.

Inexplicably and without apology, CJ's had been designated as suburban Omaha's unofficial game-day headquarters for Cleveland Browns supporters. This baffled Reginald, as Cleveland was perennially among the worst teams in the NFL. How did so many Cleveland Browns fans find their way to this pocket of suburban Omaha? It didn't make sense. Cleveland was 800 miles away in Ohio. Then again, this was Nebraska, where sporting loyalties often defied geographical logic.

The first wave of Cleveland Browns fans arrived around the time Reginald switched on the shop's OPEN sign. Decked out in burnt orange and seal brown, they were there early to stake out prime real estate in front of the big screen TV and pre-drink themselves into a stupor before kickoff. They were there to cheer on their beloved Cleveland Browns as they went head-to-head against their arch-rivals, the Pittsburgh Steelers, on ESPN's Super Sunday Game of the Week.

Reginald had little time for the empty pageantry of pro football. He considered it an unwelcome distraction from his professional objectives, namely securing promotion to the ranks of Sub-Works management. He narrowed his eyes at the sight unfolding before him in Cornhusker Plaza, noting with dismay the abject disregard these Browns fans showed toward carpark etiquette. What on earth was wrong with these people? Did societal norms mean nothing to them?

Cornhusker Plaza management had allocated each tenant a certain number of parking spaces for their exclusive use. These spaces were clearly delineated on the plaza's sun-bleached asphalt in bold yellow paint. The day-old bakery had its own allocated spaces, the flower shop had its own allocated spaces, and so on. Plenty of spaces were available in front of CJ's Poop Deck, yet carfuls of Browns fans were parking willy-nilly wherever they wanted, including spaces designated for Sub-Works customers only.

•

Reginald seethed with aggravation. Sunday was traditionally among the most lucrative days of the week at the Cornhusker Plaza Sub-Works. How were customers supposed to stop in for their delicious, made-to-order sandwiches when the carpark was overflowing with these unwashed Cleveland Browns fans? Discerning customers would surely take their business elsewhere. It sickened him to think a stupid football game would be allowed to jeopardise the bottom line at the highest-grossing Sub-Works in greater Omaha.

It was imperative that something be done. By taking bold, decisive action to protect profits through this crisis, Reginald could make a case to Sub-Works management that he was ready to lead. His heart palpitated with demented excitement as he concocted a sure-fire plan to end the anarchy that was spiralling out of control in the Cornhusker Plaza carpark.

In the office, Reginald sank into the manager's chair. He rummaged through the drawers for the phone book. In a moment he interpreted as divine providence, it opened to the listing for A-1 towing services. He dialled the number and impatiently navigated a long series of prompts. Eventually, he was connected to an human voice.

"I've got a situation here," explained Reginald. "Parking chaos. At least a dozen vehicles illegally parked at Cornhusker Plaza. Sedans. Minivans. Pickup trucks. A coupe, a few sport utility vehicles. I need all of them out of here before the situation gets any worse."

The operator spoke with a southern drawl. "Sounds like you're in a real pickle."

"I'm not one for hyperbole, but if not rectified this could escalate into bedlam. Peoples livelihoods are at stake here. Sandwich sales are in the toilet. How are people supposed to feed their families wholesome and delicious Sub-Works footlongs if they can't find a parking spot at Sub-Works?"

"I reckon I can get a couple trucks headed your way," said the operator after a long pause. "Ain't but three guys on the clock right now."

"Please," begged Reginald. "Any resources you can commit would be greatly appreciated."

"I'll see what I can do."

"You're supposed to be A-1 towing, the first name in the industry. I gotta say, your lack of enthusiasm doesn't inspire much confidence."

"Like I said, there ain't but three guys on the clock right now," said the operator, growing terse. "It's not like I'm some magician who can pull a fleet of tow trucks out of my ass. I told you I'll see what I can do. If that's not good enough, you can call Flat Top Tony's Towing and he's gonna tell you to piss off."

"I don't want to call Flat Top Tony. I just want these cars out of here."

"That's what I thought. Now just leave it to me and I'll see what I can do. First trucks should be headed your way within the hour."

With a resolution to the parking crisis in sight, Reginald allowed himself a moment of relaxation. He put the phone back in its cradle and surveyed his environs. The desk was littered with crumpled invoices and scraps of paper scrawled with names and phone numbers. What a mess. The state of the place was appalling. When he became a full-fledged manager he'd raise standards. He'd see to it that the desk was in a constant state of tidiness.

He pushed the mess to one side and put his feet up. He was overcome with a swelling sense of pride and belonging. Here, in the managers office, was where he envisioned his future, doing the important work of management. From haggling with suppliers over the price of tomatoes and bell peppers to implementing new policies for his stable of sandwich artisans to adhere to. This was the job he was born to do.

The financial compensation was another bonus. Sub-Works managers earned fifty cents more per hour than the most experienced sandwich artisans. What comfort could he bring to his life with all that extra money? The thought of finally being able to afford basic cable made him giddy.

The trance was broken by the doorbell. Its distinctive chime signalled that a customer had entered the restaurant. It triggered a Pavlov's Dog response in the sector of Reginald's medulla oblongata responsible for providing first-class customer service. Within seconds he was at the sandwich counter, greeting his customer with a hearty Sub-Works hello.

"What can I work up for you?" he asked as he scrubbed his hands in the tiny sink behind the sandwich counter.

"Let's see," said the customer, a wide-hipped woman he guessed was in her late thirties or early forties.

Reginald, with eight months of sandwich artisan experience, could size up a customer instantly. She looked like the type to bring a list, and indeed she did. She produced a square of pink paper from her massive leather handbag and unfolded it deliberately, as if she could sense his building suspense.

She cleared her throat. "I need a footlong meatball sandwich on plain white bread. Then I need a Cold-Cut Stack Attack™ on wheat, plus a footlong BMW, also on wheat."

The BMW was Sub-Works top of the line sandwich. Its official name was the Big Meaty Workout, due to its ludicrous calorie count. It was never a best-seller until a clever Sub-Works marketing campaign forged a brand alliance with the German automaker. Suddenly everybody wanted to wrap their lips around a BMW.

"I'm working on it," said Reginald cheerily.

The whole Sub-Works schtick was that the sandwich artisans painstakingly hand-crafted each and every sandwich. Reginald lovingly cradled three fresh-baked loaves in the crook of his forearm and sliced a trough into each one, forming a void in which to fill with toppings. Next he pressed with remarkable dexterity golden triangles of processed American cheese into the pocket. With care and precision he built the sandwiches layer by layer, stacking a foundation of cold cuts in a figure-eight pattern to maximise surface area, therefore maximising contact with the customer's taste-buds. He applied mayonnaise and mustard with a flourish, in the scattershot style of Jackson Pollock. He scooped marinara-drenched meatballs from the hot-bar and thoughtfully drained them slightly so the bread wouldn't be soaked through by the excess marinara.

Here, at the sandwich counter, Reginald was in his element. With laser focus he transformed each sandwich into a bespoke creation, tailored to suit each individual customer's individualism. To him, each ingredient was an instrument in the arpeggio, intermingling harmoniously as the grand symphony of flavour reached its toe-curling crescendo.

"Would you like oil and vinegar on the BMW?" he asked. "I find a slight drizzle brings out the full-bodied character of the tomatoes."

She flashed a fraudulent smile. "No thanks."

"How about a liberal dusting of salt and pepper?"

She cut him off before he could extol the flavour-enhancing properties of Sub-Works proprietary blend of Himalayan sea salt and Andalusian cracked peppercorn.

"I'm kind of in a hurry. Can we fast forward to the part where I trade you money for sandwiches?"

"No problem," said Reginald, through clenched teeth. It cheesed him off big-time when customers failed to appreciate his expertise.

He swallowed a snarky retort and proceeded to roll up the footings in wax paper. This step was crucial to the customer experience. The sandwiches needed to be rolled tight enough to keep everything in place yet not so tight as to squeeze anything out of the topping pocket.

Again, he scrubbed his hands, taking great care to work the soap into the spaces between his fingers. Despite washing them 500 times in a typical shift, the stink of onion lingered on his fingertips. It was Sub-Works policy to wash hands before handling money, but not for the hygienic reasons one might expect. Tellers at Second First Bank of Greater Omaha, where Sub-Works had its account, had complained about the stink of onions that often accompanied its cash deposits.

The buttons on the cash register bleeped and blooped as Reginald keyed in her order.

"Your total is $11.96," he said, segueing shamelessly into his up-sell pitch. Most sandwich artisans didn't bother with this rigamarole but Reginald was management material. His interactions at the point of sale were crucial to driving profits. "For just 99 cents more I can throw in three of our ooey-gooey double fudge cookies."

The woman bristled at his crass huxterism. "No thanks," she said, forking over a twenty dollar bill. "I just want to pay for my sandwiches and go."

Reginald held up the note for further inspection, as per Sub-Works policy. A poster in the food prep area warned employees of counterfeit bills and showed how to spot one. He reached in the cash drawer for a special pen with which he drew a line on the twenty dollar bill, right across Andrew Jackson's gargantuan forehead. If it was counterfeit the special ink would turn bright red. This one happened to be genuine.

Palpably disappointed, Reginald counted the woman's change back to her. His spiel continued as she impatiently checked her watch.

"It's Double-Punch Sunday. Have you heard about the Sub-Works loyalty card? Your purchase today leaves you three punches away from a free footlong of your choice on your next visit to any participating Sub-Works location in the greater Omaha area."

"Not interested in any punches," she said, in a tone of great exasperation. "Can I please just have my sandwiches?"

Another satisfied customer.

As the woman left, Reginald retreated to the back room, where his co-worker Jeffrey was reading a comic book.

"You get the next one," he said.

Jeffrey was widely regarded as Sub-Works's laziest employee. He had a bad habit of disappearing to the walk-in cooler to smoke weed during the dinner rush, leaving the rest of the team short handed at the sandwich counter. The secret of his longevity, in a word, was nepotism. Jeffrey was the owner's nephew and therefore immune from discipline.

"If you say so," said Jeffrey.

Reginald took his seat at the manager's desk and sipped from his Dr. Pepper. Free unlimited fountain sodas were among the perks of working at Sub-Works. One of his friends who worked at Long John Silver's complained that employees were charged full price for anything other than water.

The bell rang and Jeffrey reluctantly sauntered to the sandwich counter to assist the incoming customer. Reginald watched his movements on the closed-circuit system. He had the body language of someone who'd rather be doing anything but making sandwiches on a Sunday afternoon.

Reginald looked at his watch. The tow-trucks were due any minute now. He eased into the plush faux-leather manager's chair, visualising his future as a Sub-Works manager, making the schedules and ordering the weekly produce from wholesale companies. He was determined to learn all aspects of the business and maybe, with a little luck, become a Sub-Works franchisee himself.

The bell rang again. Jeffrey's glacial pace of service was causing a queue. It was up to Reginald to ensure that customers were being served promptly and effectively. He straightened out his visor and apron and joined Jeffrey at the sandwich counter.

"What can I work up for you?" he asked as he washed his hands yet again.

"Footlong steak and cheese, double the meat and add bacon," said an extremely tall man with round-framed glasses. He looked like John Lennon if John Lennon was a professional basketball player.

"White or wheat bread?"

"White."

Reginald carved a trough into a fresh loaf of bread, dipped the slotted spoon into the steak mixture, and waited as the steak brine drained off. Without that crucial step, the sandwich would become soggy, potentially creating a dissatisfied customer. He packed the meat into the bread, topped it with four slices of pre-cooked bacon and eight triangles of cheese.

"Any toppings?"

"Put some mayonnaise on there, a big handful of jalapeño peppers, and then drench the meat with red vinegar. You'll know you got it right when the bread turns pink."

As a sandwich artisan, Reginald never judged his customers, even when they presented him with bizarre topping requests. He smiled like a happy lunatic and did exactly what he was told, no matter how viscerally repulsive their requests struck him personally.

When the bread blushed pink Reginald cut the sandwich in half. He hoisted it onto a stack of wax paper and wrapped it snugly. Through the lobby windows he watched as an armada of tow trucks descended on the Cornhusker Plaza parking lot. His pulse quickened. He quickly washed his hands, keyed the order into the cash register, counted out the change, and punched his loyalty card.

Another satisfied customer.

"Jeffrey," he barked. "Next one's yours."

Reginald watched from the Sub-Works lobby with awe at the spectacle he had set into motion. The tow truck drivers worked methodically, securing illegally parked vehicles to their equipment with heavy chains and hoisting them onto two wheels with a big hydraulic arm. A baby blue Chrysler LeBaron was the first to go, followed by a forest green Pontiac Spitfire and a rusty orange Ford Bronco II.

The timing couldn't have been worse. The game had reached halftime. A restless Cleveland Browns fan stepped into the carpark to stretch his legs and was confronted with the sight of cars being towed. The man ducked back into CJ's Poop Deck and emerged moments later with an army of drunken Cleveland Browns supporters. They poured into the parking lot, shouting at the tow truck drivers.

He watched nervously as the chaos unfolded. A man in a vintage Bernie Kosar jersey grabbed one of the tow truck drivers by the lapels of his coveralls and slammed him against a minivan. Reginald stepped out onto the sidewalk to hear what they were saying.

"What the hell is going on?"

"I'm just doing my job, man," said the tow truck driver. "We got a call about some illegally parked vehicles here at the plaza and my boss sent us here to tow them away."

"I've got no beef with you, seeing as you're just doing your job," said the guy in the Bernie Kosar jersey, loosening his grip on the tow truck driver. "I give you my assurances that these cars are parked in accordance with the rules and regulations of Cornhusker Plaza."

"There's obviously been some sort of mix-up," said the tow truck driver.

"You seem like a reasonable man," said the guy in the Bernie Kosar jersey. "I propose we find a mutually agreeable solution to this little quandary. How about you and your colleagues unhitch these vehicles, and point us to whoever it was that called your company?"

"Under normal circumstances we're not allowed to share that information, but since we're all being so reasonable I suppose I can make an exception."

The circle of Cleveland Browns fans leaned in, sensing blood in the water. A moment of silence elapsed and the guy in the Bernie Kosar jersey tightened his grip.

"Tell us who called you before I get angry."

The tow truck closed his eyes and pointed across the parking lot at Reginald.

Instantly, the collective rage of the Cleveland Browns supporters was redirected from the fleet of tow truck drivers to the gangly teenager gawking at them from underneath the Sub-Works awning.

"GET HIS ASS!"

The angry mob lurched into motion, triggering Reginald's fight or flight response. He dashed back into the restaurant, pulled the chain that turned off the OPEN sign, and sprinted to the backroom for the door keys.

Jeffrey looked up from his comic book. "What's wrong, dude?"

"We're about to get a beatdown from some pissed-off Cleveland Browns fans. Get on the phone and call the cops or our asses are gonna be skin."

Reginald grabbed the keys and sprinted back to the lobby. Adrenaline flowing, he somersaulted across the sandwich counter and turned the key in the lock just before the mob reached the front door. Cleveland Browns fans foamed at the mouth as they pounded on the windows and tugged at the door, showering Reginald with vile epithets.

"Open up, you little cocksucker," shouted a short balding man with a moustache. "We're about to park a goddamn tow truck up your fucking ass when we get hold of you!"

"I'll tear you apart myself, you miserable little shit!"

Reginald shrugged at the half-drunk mob, smugly mouthing the words 'sorry, we're closed,' when his peripheral vision picked up a projectile hurtling at the storefront. A split-second later, there was a crash and the plate glass window spiderwebbed. Reginald turned and ran to the backroom, hoping Jeffrey had the police on the line, but he had disappeared.

"I've really fucked up this time," he said to himself. "There's nothing I can do except take my beating with dignity."

Ready to surrender himself to the churning throng, Reginald walked slowly and calmly back into the lobby, hands held high over his head in a posture of surrender. Just as he reached to unlock the door he heard the wailing sirens of police cruisers growing closer. Not wanting to take their chances with Omaha's finest, and their finely-calibrated breathalysers, the drunken mob scattered.

Reginald surveyed the scene. Aside from the broken window panel, there was no significant damage to the restaurant. The police arrived and offered their assistance, but Reginald declined to file a report. It was all a misunderstanding, he said, and since nobody was hurt there was no need to get the law involved. The police handed him a business card and left, happy to be spared the paperwork.

Reginald sat down at the manager's desk, resting his face in his hands. Just an hour ago, he was on the fast track to management, but his attempt at proactive decision making almost got himself killed. What would he say to his boss?

The walk-in cooler door popped open, jolting Reginald out of his thoughts. Jeffrey emerged, red-eyed and shivering from the cold.

"Is everything okay? I called the cops just like you said."

"They showed up just in time."

"I also called my uncle," said Jeffrey. "He said he's gonna send someone down here to board up the window. They'll replace the glass Tuesday."

"Was he pissed off?"

"Let's just say he wasn't thrilled to be interrupted on the golf course. He wanted me to tell you he's not gonna fire you, but you need to stop doing stupid shit like calling in tow trucks. Those guys at the sports bar are our customers too, and it's gonna take a lot of effort to win them back after that stunt you pulled today."

Reginald hadn't thought of it that way. He hung his head.

"Keep your chin up, Reggie," said Jeffrey. "Come smoke a joint with me in the walk-in cooler and I promise by the end of the day you'll realise there's more to life than making stupid sandwiches for stupid people."

Twenty years later, as he watched the fat orange sun plunge into the Pacific from the soft sandy beach of a Costa Rican surf resort, smoking a spliff like a fat cigar, Reginald— bronzed from decades of living an endless summer— reflected on that fateful Sunday at Sub-Works. Jeffery's sage advice and sweet sticky cheebah were a catalyst. In the aftermath of the tow truck fiasco he recalibrated his priorities. Why live to work when you can live for the sake of living?

THE FUNERAL DANCER

My roommate Allison was out of town, attending a feminist symposium in the forest. Probably howling at the moon with other feral women with unshaven armpits in a celebration of their collective menstrual prowess. Noelle and I had her West Asheville bungalow to ourselves. Our extended fuck-fest only paused for meal breaks and the occasional puff on a marijuana cigarette.

Spring was transitioning to summer. That magical time when bumblebees got drunk on bottomless nectar. When rivers and streams swelled with rainbow trout and bullfrogs croaked out their rustic melodies. When songbirds composed alternate lyrics to songs they've sung for centuries. When tree leaves actively reached skyward to catch the golden sunlight. It was a season of limitless possibility.

Noelle and I had chemistry. When in close proximity I could feel a charge in the air. Our pheromones fell into harmony, triggering an involuntary pituitary response which released a pyroclastic cocktail of dopamine, serotonin, and oxytocin into the bloodstream. This manifested itself as lust. As wonderful as this connection seemed on paper, its volatility posed some practical challenges.

One example was our attempt to pan-fry rainbow trout. We turned our backs on the cooktop and almost burned Allison's house down. Chemistry took over and we found ourselves caught up in the throes of spontaneous lovemaking. When the fire alarm went off we dashed into the kitchen, naked, slicked with fuck-sweat, choking on black smoke. Our wild-caught trout fillets were aflame in my roommate's antique cast iron skillet. I had no idea where she kept the fire extinguisher. I shouted for Noelle to check the cabinets. Flustered, she suggested that we call 911.

"The last thing we need is a visit from the fire department," I said. "Whatever happens, we can't let Allison find out about this."

I removed the skillet from the burner. Like an absolute imbecile, I placed it under the faucet. A massive fireball erupted from the pan. It climbed the stonework backsplash and kissed the ceiling before flaming out. Only dumb luck prevented anything else from igniting, aside from my eyelashes and eyebrows which had been singed out of existence.

We opened the windows to air the place out, trading black smoke for crisp mountain air. The ceiling was blackened with soot from the fireball. A fresh coat of paint and my roommate would be none the wiser. Her antique cast-iron skillet, on the other hand, would almost certainly require re-seasoning. I could picture Allison lamenting my mistreatment of her precious family heirloom, but that was tomorrow's problem. Noelle and I needed caloric sustenance after our harrowing misadventure. We popped out to Universal Joint, my local pub, for stiff drinks and crispy tater tots.

●

I learned her full name from court documents—Noelle Louise Lacoste. She grabbed headlines that spring for her role in an bizarre incident across the border in South Carolina. She showed up uninvited to a stranger's funeral, where she had some sort of psychotic meltdown. According to court documents she broke the antennae off a parked car and waltzed into Sunny Side Up Baptist Church as the funeral was taking place. As the organist played funeral hymns, Noelle pirouetted about the sanctuary, waving the antennae like a magic wand.

Initially, attendees accepted her antics as part of the ceremony. She carried on dancing without protest. But as her performance escalated to a crescendo it became obvious that something was amiss. Noelle approached the open casket, gyrating her hips in a pseudo-sexual manner before waving her wand over the dead man's body. She tapped him on the forehead and shouted 'I love you' three times before hoisting a floral arrangement into the air and heaving it towards horrified friends and family members of the deceased.

That's when all hell broke loose.

In the ensuing chaos, amidst the wails of distraught funeral goers, Noelle managed to escape. Eluding lunging pallbearers, she scurried out a side door and into the parking lot where she fled the scene in her burgundy Toyota. A clergyman took down the license number and called police. Noelle was apprehended by Clementine County Sheriff's deputies a short time later. The media picked up the story and ran with it. From then on, Noelle would forever be known as The Funeral Dancer.

One thing about Noelle is that she has a lazy eye. It's her most prominent feature and probably explains why, in written statements to police, witnesses described her as looking deranged. That droopy-eyed visage was captured for posterity in the Clementine County Sheriff's official booking photograph. The mugshot, once published, was instantly iconic, and earned The Funeral Dancer multiple mentions in late-night talk show monologues. Noelle had achieved pop cultural infamy.

My curiosity was piqued. I had an overwhelming urge to meet this young woman. Someone needed to tell her side of the story, and I was convinced I was the right man for the job.

I eventually found myself face-to-face with the Noelle, The Funeral Dancer, in a dimly-lit booth at a vegan cafe in downtown Asheville where a bunch of dusty hippies had prepared seventeen bean soup in a massive cauldron. But I wasn't there for soup. I was there to finally hear the fascinating story of her psychotic episode in granular detail. But when it mattered most from a journalistic point of view, Noelle Louise Lacoste eluded me.

•

A slow news day was abruptly interrupted by the high-pitched whine of Assignment Editor Jeremiah Crisp. Within the newsroom he was regarded as mildly annoying, moderately competent, and thoroughly non-threatening. Outside the newsroom he was a model train enthusiast who, when dressed in women's clothing, was a doppelgänger for Mrs. Doubtfire.

"We need someone on this," crowed Jeremy. "Who in their right mind would dance around the casket and throw flowers at a stranger's funeral?"

Newsroom staff gathered around to read the press release. There was a collective gasp when the mugshot attachment was opened. There she was, Noelle Louise Lacoste, 24 years old, peering into the newsroom with her lazy eye. She had curly blonde hair worn above the shoulders. Her eyes were green. She was five-foot-four and weighed 126 pounds. She'd been charged under article seven of the South Carolina state code, section 16, for wilfully, knowingly or maliciously disturbing a funeral service. Additional charges of disorderly conduct and instigating affray were thrown in— prosecutorial icing on the cake.

"This could be our lead story," chimed in Julie Dobson, a nightside Associate Producer with a flair for profanity. "We've got jack-shit else happening tonight. I could really use a double homicide right now. What's the fucking game plan, people?"

I listened from the confines of a nearby edit suite as the newsroom came to life. A field-tested professional knows to stay out of sight until the 'indoor cats' have wrapped their heads around an unfolding news situation. Stick your neck out too early and you might find yourself in a Walmart carpark chasing man-on-the-street interviews that would never see the airwaves.

"Let's get the mugshot on the website right away." Jeremiah was breathless with excitement. "Derek and Courtney's story on the UFO sighting in Swannanoa has fallen through. We'll divert them to Clementine County to get reaction from eyewitnesses at the church. I've already texted them the address."

"I want a live shot in the goddamn A-block. From the church if possible. And if Courtney can find that motherfucking car antennae it would make for a kick-ass show-and-tell when she's in live in the double-box shot. Do we have any motherfucking journalists to chase down this crazy-ass bitch? Who can we send to find the motherfucking Funeral Dancer?"

My ears perked up. I was known for having the Midas touch when it came to convincing damaged and somewhat deranged individuals to consent to on-camera interviews. I emerged from my edit suite, like a genie from a bottle, to volunteer for the prime assignment. Equipped with a print-out of Noelle's mugshot and a last-known address, my mission was to track down the Funeral Dancer and ask her the question on everyone's mind— why the hell would you crash a stranger's funeral?

With any luck, the interview would make for some exceptionally good television. How could it not? I gathered my camera equipment and loaded into my logo-wrapped news car, clutching the Funeral Dancer's strangely fascinating mugshot and wondering if this would be the story that finally earned me an Emmy nomination.

●

Noelle's last known address was on the shores of Lake Toxaway, in the outer reaches of my station's designated market area. My GPS told me it would be a 90 minute drive. I took I-26 south out of Asheville, linked up with Highway 64 at Hendersonville, and headed west into the Blue Ridge mountains. The tree-lined highway narrowed to two lanes as it snaked through the tiny mountain hamlets of Etowah, Brevard, and Roman. The scenic vistas were marred only by the occasional billboards for bail bondsmen and fast food restaurants. I spent much of the journey boxed-in behind a slow-moving 18-wheeler laden with fresh-cut timber, breathing in pine-tar fumes. By the time I arrived at the compact, well-kept, two-storey craftsman bungalow overlooking the lake, daylight was fading fast.

It's not easy to remain inconspicuous in a vehicle emblazoned with a TV station's call letters. I parked some distance away where I could survey the scene discreetly. Things weren't looking good, my instincts told me. No cars in the driveway, no lights on in the house. If nobody was home my excursion could evolve into an hours-long stakeout or worse, a wild goose chase. I texted the assignment desk that I was at the house and preparing my approach.

It was early March. The brown grass was still waiting for the changing seasons to breathe into it new life. It felt spongy under the soles of my Sperry Top Siders as I approached to the front door. I pressed the doorbell and waited. No barking of dogs, no footsteps in the foyer, no sign of the Funeral Dancer. I opened the screen door and knocked several times on the solid hardwood door, harder than necessary. It had been painted red, like maraschino cherries. I waited and waited. No one was home.

I called the assignment desk with an update. With it being a dreadfully slow news day, it was determined that I should keep my eyes on the house.

"This is our lead story, asshole," said the ever-adamant Julie. "Stay put until you get me a motherfucking soundbite."

Anyone who thinks TV news is a glamorous profession never spent a shift on stakeout. Day turned to night, and I was still in the news car, eating granola bars and listening to a mildly interesting public radio segment about Somali pirates in the Gulf of Aden. Meanwhile, I kept my eyes peeled for any signs of Noelle Louise Lacoste and her burgundy Toyota.

I had just settled into the tedium of my stakeout when my Kyocera flip phone buzzed to life. Breaking news— a structure fire at a fraternity house in Cullowhee, an hour's drive from Lake Toxaway. The news cycle is fickle. It had moved from the Funeral Dancer onto the next soundbite-sized crisis, sweeping away my chances for an Emmy. I understood how it worked. The news beast's aching hunger must be satiated.

The fire was out by the time I arrived. I got video of firefighters packing up their hoses and a boilerplate soundbite with the Chief. Everything I needed to turn a forgettable B-block story. But a good journalist always keeps their eyes on the prize. Before I cut bait on my Lake Toxaway stakeout, I wrote a note on a scrap of paper and wedged it into the gap in the doorframe.

Salutations, Noelle—

My name is Cosmo Archer. I'm a journalist with Action 13 News. I'm curious to hear your account of what happened at Sunny Side Up Baptist Church today. There are two sides to every story. Please call me, I promise not to judge. My number is: (828) 321-2141.

•

This all happened around the time my wife Mackenzie decided she'd had enough. She had slipped into a depression after moving to Asheville and having the baby. She was too sad to work. I tried to understand where she was coming from, but couldn't. I felt like she was taking advantage of my work ethic, breaking my back as revenge for years of marital disappointment. I was frequently late for work because she refused to get out of bed to look after our two-year-old son Owen. When her grandfather was put in a nursing home, Mackenzie jumped at the chance to leave me to live rent-free in his vacated house.

I wasn't exactly sad to see her go. The relationship had been dead for a long time. But still, her departure caused me serious pain because she took our son. The timing was cruel, an intentional twisting of the knife. This particular human drama unfolded over the weekend of my 33rd birthday.

The memories will haunt me forever. The look of confusion on Owen's face as the U-Haul was being loaded. His sobs as he was strapped into the back of his mother's car. Me pressing my palm against the window, struggling to keep it together during this soul-destroying goodbye. I stood and watched the U-Haul disappear around the corner and out of my life. I found myself face-down on the living room floor, hopeless in the aftermath. I was pathetic, a shell of myself, my spirit imploded by a vacuum of utter emptiness.

Life would never be the same. The simple joys of being a parent were no longer my remit. No more chopping up fruit for Owen's breakfast. No more afternoons together at the playground. My new role was that of absentee father— sending child support checks and receiving an annual school photo in return. I felt like I'd been stripped of any purpose.

Moving on meant downsizing. I traded my two-bedroom apartment by the Grove Park Inn for a room in Allison's bungalow. My colleagues emerged as my support system and biggest cheerleaders. Nightside reporters Heather Arbuckle, Nora Eastwood, and Pasadena Potts assured me over salt-rimmed margaritas that the sting of my failed marriage would fade, and that new love lurked right around the corner. All I needed to do was let myself heal and everything else would fall into place.

I found myself receptive to their message. After five years in a joyless, sexless, dead-end relationship, I wasn't quite ready to embrace the idea of new love, but I was ready to move on. I would later find truth in the adage that the world works in mysterious ways.

●

It was my day off. Far away from the meat-grinder of television news, I browsed the aisles of La Tienda Catrachitas grocery store in search of habanero sauce for a recipe. In the weeks since my world unravelled, I found solace in cooking. I was no chef, but the act of chopping and slicing ingredients, following a recipe, and transforming them into something different seemed therapeutic. Cooking diverted my attention from the nagging existential queries that foment when one is faced with starting over from scratch.

I was fondling a massive avocado, contemplating guacamole, when my Kyocera came to life in my pants pocket. My first inkling was to ignore the unfamiliar number, but the famous quote about the definition of insanity being doing the same thing over and over but expecting different results came to mind. I made a conscious decision to break from the rigidity of my old instincts, to choose sanity over the alternative. I answered just before the call redirected to voice mail.

"Cosmo Archer speaking."

"Hi, this is Noelle, um, from the funeral. You left your number at my house a few weeks ago. I'm ready to tell my side of story if that still interests you."

More than just another story, this was a springboard to something new. The news cycle had all but forgotten The Funeral Dancer, but that didn't matter. To me, this was bigger than news. I sensed that it would expose a new path forward for me, bringing me something I'd been missing but lacked the vocabulary to articulate. Noelle and I made arrangements to meet the following week. I put down the avocado and noticed I'd squeezed it so hard I'd broken its skin.

•

In the days before my meeting with Noelle, my fascination with the Funeral Dancer story became obsessive. No longer was I concerned with its Emmy award winning potential. I needed to get inside her head to satisfy my own peace of mind. I wanted it all, the backstory, the sordid first-hand details, the emotional sub-context. I couldn't stop thinking about the Funeral Dancer. Questions swirled in my mind like blowing snow. My only worry was that Noelle would pull a no-show.

Considering her swift return to anonymity after her mugshot went viral, was it in Noelle's best interest to pick the scab? She'd be insane to reinsert her name and image into the public domain. Would it be unethical to pursue her side of story from a journalistic perspective? Did it cross the line into exploitation? As it turns out, these questions were rendered moot at the editorial meeting.

"The Funeral Dancer? Nice try, Cosmo, but that's ancient history. We need something fresh for tonight's newscast," groaned Julie. "Where was this crazy bitch three weeks ago when the world actually gave two shits about her?"

The cool reception wasn't completely discouraging. Without pressure to generate content, I could relax and be myself, unburdened by the albatross of a hard deadline. But when our meeting rolled around, I was anything but relaxed. I had the same butterflies-in-stomach feeling one might associate with first dates and job interviews.

I showered, shaved, and removed stray hair from my nostrils with a pair of rusty tweezers. I slid into my best jeans and changed shirts three times before settling on a nonthreatening striped polo. Freshly scrubbed and gleaming, my palpitating heart and I made our way to the white-hot and freaky molten core of downtown Asheville to meet Noelle Louise Lacoste, AKA the Funeral Dancer.

•

We met at the Rosetta Stoner Cafe. It was community cauldron night. A massive cast iron pot dangled from a sturdy double-arched frame, where an apron-clad woman who I presumed was Rosetta happily circulated the seventeen bean mixture with a giant wooden ladle. The premise was a hit among a certain demographic: fire-dancing vegans and hackey-sack players who eschewed basic hygiene, ingested mass quantities of off-market pharmaceuticals, and begged for spare change in Pritchard Park.

I was on-edge with the uneasy feeling that an impromptu drum circle could erupt at any moment. I slid into a purple faux-leather booth with a view of the front door, downwind from the cauldron's earthen aroma, where I ordered a glass of house-brewed Kombucha and waited for Noelle.

Preconceptions can be deceiving. It seemed unrealistic to expect a person who would crash a stranger's funeral to show up on time for an appointment, but Noelle walked through the door at exactly seven o'clock. She wore a red turtleneck sweater underneath faded blue jean overalls with holy knees and black Doc Martens. She was prettier in-person than I expected. Her glossy curls bounced with life, directing attention away from her lazy eye as she surveyed the dining room. I raised my arm to catch her attention and she joined me in the booth. After an exchange of pleasantries she began her monologue.

"I was feeling so nervous about meeting you that I considered not showing up. This whole thing with the arrest and the whirlwind of attention that came with it has been really strange. I feel like everyone is so quick to paint me like some kind of deviant, a crazy person, but I swear I'm not crazy."

If my years of experience in journalism had taught me anything, it's that if someone insists they're not crazy, they usually are. I noted this red flag as she continued.

"Part of myself wants to just forget the whole thing ever happened, plead guilty in court, take whatever punishment they hand down, pay the fine, do the community service and move on. But there's another part of me that wants to be heard. I want to be understood."

A heavily tattooed and pierced waitress interrupted to deliver another round of Kombucha.

"I almost tossed your note in the trash. No offence, but I've heard horror stories about rogue journalists taking words out of context, twisting their meanings and making things out to be what they're not. But the longer I held onto the note, the more I felt drawn to respond. After much thought, I decided to go ahead and contact you. I thought it might be therapeutic to unburden myself, to tell someone else what led up to the incident."

She opened her handbag to retrieve a folded square of paper festooned with notes and sketches. As she unfolded it, she told me she wrote out her story on paper so her thoughts would be in order when we met.

"You know, in case we are sitting here and I go blank," she explained.

The Rosetta Stoner Cafe was packed with bodies. I had never seen so many white people with dreadlocks in one place. It was surreal. There were flower children, free spirits, and indigo souls. There were bohemian couch surfers exuding ultralight beams of peace, love, and happiness, all nourishing themselves from within the seemingly-bottomless cauldron. I was in the throes of a spiritual contact high, existing simultaneously within the confines of the cafe and on a much higher plane. Noelle had accompanied me to that liminal space, I could sense it, high above the din of horoscope conversations, above the total rhubarb of background noise. Nothing mattered except the details of that day, crashing a stranger's funeral at Sunny Side Up Baptist Church. Methodically and without shame, she told me everything.

"It started off as an ordinary day. There was nothing noteworthy about it, not hot, not cold, not sunny, not cloudy. I just finished massage school and I didn't have any clients and I felt stir-crazy from doing nothing. Pure boredom. I was sick of being alone and staring out the window at Lake Toxaway. I said to myself, fuck it, why don't I go on an adventure? So that's what I did, I got in the car and started driving, randomly, with no particular destination in mind."

"That's how you ended up in South Carolina?"

"Yeah, just trying to interpret some kind of signal from the universe, following its cues, right? I had this feeling that something interesting was eventually going to happen if I just let my subatomic particles fall into line with the structure of the universe."

"Sounds intense. Like you were a conduit for the actions of the universe."

"Not so much, I mean, I was still in control of the car, driving, using my hands to physically steer the car, using my feet to press the gas and tap the brakes. It's not like I became a mindless robot. I was using turn signals at junctions, physically driving the car. I wasn't going to let myself crash under the guise of letting the universe take over. I just tried to pick up the vibrations the universe was sending and take actions that were in harmony with those vibrations."

She produced a tin of Altioids and popped one in her mouth before continuing.

"When I came upon the funeral procession and saw the long line of cars driving super slow on the highway with their headlights on, something like a voice called out to me. I was needed. Those vibrations came straight from the universe to my heart. I did the only thing that was right in that moment— I manoeuvred my car into the funeral procession and followed it to the church. I watched from the carpark as people hugged each other and cried. It was terribly sad. That's when I felt the dead man's energy inside me."

"You felt his energy?"

"Remember that movie where Drew Barrymore is a little girl who starts fires with her mind? His soul, or something, was directing kinetic energy at me, and I was simply responding to it. It was like listening to a radio broadcast, except I was the only person tuned into the right frequency. It made the hairs on the back of my neck stand up, and I felt myself getting wet between the legs."

She hesitated. A good journalist knows that most interviewees presented with silence will keep talking just to fill the void. I resisted my urge to follow up and she carried on with her narrative.

"I did what I had to do, which was the right thing. Everything they said in the news reports was accurate. I broke the antennae off a car. Kinetic energy took over and before I knew it I was inside the church, whirling and twirling to the organ music. There were supercharged electrons vibrating through me while I danced. The people in the church, their faces were blank, like they weren't really present, not in the same way I was present. They were like zombies. The only thing real was this man's energy, I heard him calling out for me and I was overwhelmed by the urge to release him, to set him free."

I scribbled furiously in my notebook, struggling to keep up with the quickening cadence as her story neared its climax.

"That's when I had the most powerful sensation. The entirety of this man's emotional being was pulsating through me, and I knew in that moment that all he ever wanted was to be loved. I opened the casket and saw him there, and I told him I loved him. This angered the people in the church and they became aggressive. They started coming at me, and that's when I threw the flowers at them. It was a defensive move. The misplaced hate and anger inside them was directed at me and I had to get away."

"Do you regret doing it? They're not felonies or anything, but you're facing all those criminal charges."

She paused for a moment, searching herself for an answer. My wrist ached from note taking, and I used the time to massage my tendons.

"I'm sorry everyone got so angry about it, but his family caused him to make this cosmic cry for help. They didn't love or appreciate him when he was still alive. A little love goes a long way in this world. I have no regrets. Like I told the Sheriff's Deputies, I did what I had to do, which was the right thing."

Having heard her explanation it seemed perfectly acceptable. Maybe she was a little crazy, but she also struck me as vulnerable and empathetic, highly sensitive to the unseen world around us, the ebb and flow of forces that exist outside the sensory perceptions of so-called normal people.

We left the Rosetta Stoner Cafe, but neither of us wanted the night to end. The conversation flowed as we walked through downtown Asheville, past the ethnic restaurants and crystal shops on Lexington Avenue, up Walnut hill past Malaprop's Bookstore, past the Thomas Wolfe Auditorium, past the towing red-brick Basilica of St.

Lawrence, past the snooty wine bars at the Grove Arcade, down Patton Avenue to the Jack of the Wood pub where we drank pitcher after pitcher of locally-brewed craft beer.

I woke up the next morning, naked, with Noelle in my arms. I was overcome with the warm and fuzzy sensation of well-being. It was as if I'd undergone some kind of transformation. My body and spirit felt clean and pure, rejuvenated. Was this what it felt like to be born again? Noelle snuggled into me and I called in sick.

•

We became a casual item after that, meeting for drinks after work and having unprotected sex in cars, restaurant bathrooms, and in wide open fields under the bright summer sun. The photovoltaic bond we forged was thrilling but unsustainable. Our combustible chemistry reached its crescendo with that fiery explosion in Allison's kitchen. Like a child playing with matches, the attraction was in knowing that everything would go up in flames.

For a brief moment were like twin stars, revolving around each other, dancing in the gravitational forces that surrounded us. It was a material exchange. I was the sympathetic ear, listening without judgement and validating her exuberant individuality. What others might dismiss as mental illness, I viewed as the central aspect of her being. Noelle was uniquely attenuated to the energy of the universe. She had the empath's ability to register the subtle vibrations of human suffering.

The more I think about it, the more I believe Noelle was sent to fix me. She was tuned into my frequency. She could sense I was a wounded animal and responded in kind to my emotional distress signals. In the short time we were together, the trajectory of my life changed for the better.

Noelle was like a bolt of lightning that shocked me out of my stagnancy. She offered an escape from heartbreak and my inevitable descent into self-flagellation. Like the man at the funeral, part of me was already dead— or dying— until she answered my cosmic cries for help. Her intervention saved me from my own bitterness. She flattered me, fulfilling my desperate need for female attention and nourishing my fragile male ego when I needed it most.

When I had regained the strength to survive outside the cool cocoon of our couplehood, Noelle was in the wind.

SOME NEXT LEVEL SHIT

It started in the pandemic with a Facebook post. I clicked the link, entered my bank details, and just like that we had a milkman.

The milkman delivered on Tuesdays and Saturdays. He did his round super early in the morning, left the milk waiting on the doorstep. I worried hedgehogs might scurry off with it, but that never happened. We ordered two large cartons of blue low-fat milk and occasionally a carton of red full-fat milk. The red milk was especially decadent when poured over cereal.

Having a milkman was some next level shit. No more popping out and dealing with mask-wearing regulations, one-way systems, and extra-long queues just for a quart of milk. The milkman had us covered.

One day, the milkman included a flyer with our delivery. He was expanding his offerings to include yoghurt, eggs, cheese, and butter.

My wife was working from home. "This is amazing," she said.

"I know," I said. "We're one step closer to never having to leave this place."

Together we scrawled out a list. Two packets of salted butter. A couple raspberry yoghurts. Half a dozen double-yolk eggs. We even splurged on expensive smoked cheddar because it felt good to support the local farming community.

The milkman took orders via Facebook messenger. I sent the order and he responded immediately.

"Hey baby-cakes," I hollered to my wife. "Our order is in. The milkman says 'K'."

"Having a milkman is some next level shit," she said. "There's nothing like waking up to a fuck-tonne of dairy on your doorstep."

Both of us woke up before the alarm. We were too excited to sleep.

"Did you hear something?" she whispered. "I think it was the front gate."

"Could it be the milkman?"

We put on dressing gowns to investigate. The milkman had made his delivery.

"Hold on, baby-cakes," I said. "This is a moment worth remembering. Let me get my phone so I can get a picture for Instagram."

My wife went back upstairs to get dressed while I made breakfast. I was unreasonably excited about the double-yolk eggs, laid by freak hens or something. Two yolks every time. This was really some next level shit.

The situation cried out for omelettes. I chopped up mushrooms, onions, and peppers and heated coconut oil in the pan. So what if there was a lockdown and we couldn't leave the house. We had a milkman.

The eggs weren't exactly what I expected. They were gigantic, with lovely orange double yolks, but nobody had bothered to wipe the chicken shit from the shells. I was horrified. Even under a hot water scrub the shit wouldn't come off.

"How are the eggs," said my wife. "Do they really have double yolks?"

"These local farmers are taking the piss," I said. "These eggs cost twice as much as regular eggs from the store, but they couldn't be bothered to wipe the chicken shit off the shells?"

"Disgusting."

"I'll crack them carefully so we don't get bits of poo in our omelettes."

At some point the milkman became part of the new normal everyone was going on about. The novelty of dairy on our doorstep wore off gradually as we realised the milkman was kind of an asshole.

He brought us too much butter one morning and refused to take it back. All of a sudden we were in possession of an alarming quantity of butter. We stacked packets of butter like bricks in the back of the fridge. The milkman didn't answer my Facebook messages so I rang him on the telephone. I tried to stay calm but I was fired up. My heart was beating like hummingbird wings.

"What am I supposed to do with all this goddamn butter?" I shouted into my phone. "I've got a cholesterol problem, what are you trying to do, kill me? Are you a milkman, or are you a murderer?"

My wife enjoys when I freak out at people over the phone. "The best part was that milkman or murderer line," she said after the call. "It was almost poetic."

"Lock him up," I joked. "The milkman murdered my love for omelettes with his shit-covered eggs."

We decided to give the milkman another chance. Maybe there were crossed wires in the supply chain. Maybe we got somebody else's order by mistake. These unprecedented times had softened us, made us sentimental for simpler things.

But the milkman turned out to be a bigger asshole than we first thought. This time, he delivered the appropriate amount of butter, but mangled our yoghurt order.

"Lemon yoghurt?" I said. "I can't choke that down."

"Unacceptable," said my wife. "He's been our milkman for two months. He should know by now we only like raspberry yoghurt."

It was time to cut the milkman loose.

Part of me wanted to call him up, to rip him a new asshole, but I just couldn't summon the rage. It's not good for one's mental health to get worked up over a simple prick. Instead I sent a Facebook message, letting him know his services were no longer needed.

My wife wanted to know how the milkman handled the news.

"Classic milkman," I said. "He just said 'K'."

THE DROUGHT OF 1995

Chris Baxter was the new guy at Sub-Works Sandwich Factory. He had a head like a cube and bushy caterpillar eyebrows. He drove a rusted out Chevrolet Chevette with Iowa plates. He was from Dubuque and worked that fact into practically every conversation.

"Back in Dubuque we used to huff paint thinner by the riverbank," he told me as we we sliced vegetables together at the prep table. "Then we'd go over to Spider's house and listen to Butthole Surfers on acid."

"Oh yeah?"

"There was always rad shit happening in Dubuque."

I tried not to be defensive. "Omaha's cool too."

"It's alright," he said, feeding bell peppers into the crank slicer. "But back home in Dubuque it was easier to get drugs."

For reasons beyond our understanding drugs had become scarce. Even small quantities of pot, normally cheap and plentiful, were unavailable. What a time to be alive— bored stiff and living through the drought of 1995 on minimum wage.

"It can't stay dry forever."

"I hope you're right because I'm losing my fucking mind here. Back in Dubuque there were hot girls. Nebraska girls are pug-ugly."

Girls from either state weren't lining up to fuck us. Who wants a guy who works for minimum wage and reeks of onions?

Chris offered to drive me home after work, but the Chevette wouldn't start. Instead of walking for help at the 7-11 down the block we smoked cigarettes in the parking lot, waiting for someone to drive by for a jump start.

"I'm so fucking desperate to get high," said Chris.

"I can check in with my weed guy again," I offered. "He told me he was hoping to get a quarter pound of dank buds sometime soon."

"Call that motherfucker!"

No luck. Omaha was the epicentre of a new dust bowl.

Chris stood on the edge of the road, waving his jumper cables at passing cars. Eventually a guy in a Ford F-150 pulled in to help, a wispy, no-nonsense older gentleman with tightly furrowed wrinkles. He popped open the hood of his truck, and five minutes later Chris and I were in the Taco Bell drive-thru listening to The Melvins on the Chevette's tinny speakers.

"These guys played the Capitol Bar a few months ago."

"I've lost count of how many times I've seen The Melvins," said Chris. "Dubuque is practically their second home."

We ordered burritos and ate in the carpark.

•

There was nothing to do after that, so we drove around in circles. They called it cruising— the thing to do when there was nothing else to do. Carfuls of hopelessly sober midwestern teenagers going out of their minds in the drought of 1995.

"Back in Dubuque there were bonfires every Saturday night," said Chris. "We'd get cases of Keystone Light and drink until we puked."

"I can't wait until I'm 21 so I can get drunk."

"My older brother Kenny used to buy us beer. Now he's in jail."

"What'd he do?"

"Armed robbery. Three years for supposedly being the lookout. The fucking judge railroaded his ass. That's why I'm here. I used to live with Kenny but when he went to prison I came to live with my Aunt and Uncle."

"Fucking Christ."

Chris accelerated through a yellow light the instant before it turned red and pulled into the Walgreens parking lot at the top of the hill.

"I gotta get fucked up tonight," he said. "Are you with me?"

"I wanna get fucked up too."

"Have you ever taken Robitussin? It's cough medicine, but if you drink the entire bottle real fast time slows down and you end up tripping balls."

"From Robitussin?"

"Yeah, but it's got to be the kind that says DM on the package. The active ingredient is hallucinogenic."

"How much should we take?"

"Two bottles each should put us in another dimension."

Chris sent me in to the Pharmacy. I found the Robitussin in the cough and cold aisle. I inspected each package carefully to ensure we were getting the highest possible dosage of the active ingredient. I put the Robitussin in a hand basket along with a bag of Werther's Originals and a copy of Guns & Ammo magazine.

"Is that everything for you?" said the woman at checkout.

I nodded. The woman scanned the magazine and the candies, but paused when she saw four boxes of Robitussin DM.

"I'm afraid I can only sell you two boxes of cough syrup at a time."

"Why is that?"

"It's flagged as a frequently abused item."

"Look, I'm Mormon. I'm the oldest of eight siblings and we've got a bug going around right now, terrible stuff. I got sent out for medicine because I haven't got the cough yet."

The clerk folded her arms across her chest. She wasn't buying the story.

"You're Mormon?"

"Yes ma'am," I said. "I just want to do right for my brothers and sisters. I don't want to see them wheezing like a bunch of broken down accordions. I shouldn't even be here, because I've potentially been exposed to whatever is causing the cough. If you help me out, I'll add your name to our daily prayer list."

She scanned the remaining boxes. "Fine, but if I catch you buying any psychoactive cough syrup here again I will call the authorities. We take over-the-counter medicine abuse very seriously."

"Thank you, I could tell you were one of God's people."

•

I gave Chris a thumbs-up and got back in the car. As he drove us to his aunt and uncle's house on the edge of town I told him about how the clerk bought my Mormon sob story.

"That's brilliant," he said. "Back in Dubuque the pharmacies could be dicks about buying more than one package of Robitussin. Sometimes we'd have to go to two or three different stores to get enough to get fucked up on."

"You should've seen her face when I told her I was going to put her name on my prayer list. Her eyes nearly popped out of her skull."

Chris pulled into the driveway at his aunt and uncle's split-level house but no one was home.

"They go to the casino on Friday night," he explained as he unlocked the front door.

He led me down a half-flight of stairs into a shag carpeted recreation room. The wood panelling and velvet Elvis painting were relics of the 1970's. Also in the room was a large stereo system, a dartboard, a red lava lamp, a bear's head rug, a glass coffee table, and two plush leather sofas that had seen better days.

"Whatcha think?"

"This place is fucking awesome. Who killed the bear?"

"Nobody. My uncle got it at a flea market. I don't think it's real."

"Either way, it's badass."

Chris loaded a Primus CD into the stereo. Les Claypool's bass-lines sounded ferocious on his uncle's top-of-the-line Bose speakers. He brought two glasses of water and a large plastic bowl down from the kitchen.

"Ready to trip your balls off?"

"Bring it on."

We each opened a box of Robitussin and cracked through the child-proof safety caps.

"You'll want to drink it fast, but not too fast because it might make you puke. It's supposed to be raspberry flavoured, but it tastes like human shit. If you throw up, make sure you get it in the bowl and not on the carpet. My uncle will beat my ass if I fuck up his carpet."

Chris tossed back his cube-shaped head and chugged. Then it was my turn. The Robitussin was thick and sickly sweet. I drank half the bottle and felt the urge to vomit. I grabbed the bowl, but kept it down. Chris was already cracking the cap on his second bottle.

"This shit is nasty," I said.

"It will be worth it when you're drooling into the carpet."

I got the first bottle down and started on my second. I felt myself drifting into an altered state. At first it was a ringing in my ears, like a nitrous oxide buzz, but soon it started to impact my perception of the room. Time slowed down. Objects in my field of vision appeared shimmery and distorted, as if I was looking at everything through a rippling wall of water. My motor skills failed and I found myself, as predicted, drooling into the carpet, face-to-face with the taxidermy bear's toothy grin. I was so close I could see plaque on its long sharp teeth.

"I'm so fucked up," said Chris. "I feel like my heart's gonna stop."

I started laughing. The Robitussin made everything seem funny.

"This isn't funny, dude, I think I'm fucking dying."

I pushed myself up onto my hands and knees and crawled over to him. He was face down and convulsing in the shag carpet. His skin was pale and grey like aliens in movies.

"You should make yourself puke."

"I never had to make myself puke back in Dubuque."

"You might feel better. Lemme get the bowl."

I crawled slowly through the thick carpet. It seemed like it was alive and growing taller. I pictured amber waves of grain as I retrieved the bowl from the coffee table.

"Here," I said. "Puke into this."

"You're a demon and you're trying to fuck with my head just like you did back in Dubuque." Chris started crying. His trip was going all wrong.

"I'm Jason from Sub-Works, remember? Not some demon. We work together making sandwiches."

Chris pushed himself up onto his knees. His eyes rolled back in his head. The Robitussin had sent him over the edge and now he was completely unhinged.

"Devil, I cast thee out of this house!" he shouted. "I smote thee with my righteous fury! I condemn thee to eternal damnation!"

"You're killing my buzz," I slapped him across the face. "Get yourself together, man, it's just a bad trip."

Chris collapsed on the shag carpet and sobbed into his hands.

"Why does this always happen to me?"

"If you make yourself puke you'll feel better."

I slid the bowl across the carpet. Chris leaned over it and stuck his fingers deep into his throat. He dry-heaved a couple times before it came up, in short hot bursts. Pieces of tomato and lettuce from his burrito floated in a sea of raspberry Robitussin. The Taco Bell carpark seemed like ancient history.

"That's it, get it all out," I said. "Doesn't that feel better?"

Chris looked at me. His eyes were watery and stomach acids oozed from his nose, but he looked better, as if the worst part of the trip was over.

"Where am I?"

"You're at your aunt and uncle's house in Omaha."

"Am I dead?"

"You look like death but you're still alive."

"I miss Dubuque."

Chris eventually mellowed out. Without having to babysit, I could finally relax and enjoy the psychotropic effects of Robitussin.

I put Jane's Addiction on the stereo and flipped through my copy of Guns & Ammo, wondering what it would be like to shoot a human head. Would it explode like a watermelon at a Gallagher show, or would the bullet tunnel through and exit from the back of the head? I contemplated the physics as Chris's aunt and uncle returned from the casino.

"What the hell is going on here?" demanded Chris' uncle. "Turn down the goddamn stereo and answer me."

"He invited me over to listen to music," I gestured at Chris, who was writhing face-down on the carpet and giggling uncontrollably. "We work together at Sub-Works and we like a lot of the same bands."

The uncle surveyed the room. Four empty bottles of Robitussin DM and a large plastic bowl of vomit sat on the glass coffee table. He shook his head.

"Drinking Robitussin?"

I shrugged. "It's not as bad as it sounds."

"This shit fucks you up," said Chris. "The devil chased me here all the way from Dubuque!"

"You haven't been huffing paint again, have you?" His uncle was obviously exasperated. "You've already been to rehab once for solvent abuse."

"Rehab?" said Chris. "Fuck that place."

"He's only had Robitussin, that I know of."

"Get your things" the uncle told me. "I'll drive you home."

The presence of reasonable adults sobered me quickly. I climbed into the passenger seat of the uncle's Dodge Ram and buckled my seatbelt.

"Where's your place?"

"Just drop me off at Sub-Works," I said. "My parents will kill me if I come home tripping on Robitussin. I have a key to the store and can sleep in the back on the prep table."

"You seem like a good kid. Why are you hanging out with a guy like Chris?"

"I don't know, he seems okay."

"He's got a lot of problems," said the uncle. "Ever since his brother went to prison we've been trying to give him some structure in his life."

"He said his brother was railroaded, that he was just the lookout."

"That's what Chris wants to believe. He loves his brother, but the truth is Kenny was a bad dude. He got in over his head on amphetamines and started robbing gas stations to feed his habit."

The uncle pulled into the Sub-Works parking lot.

"It would probably be for the best if you stopped hanging around Chris. I'm afraid he might be going down his brother's path."

•

I woke up hours later in the back room of Sub-Works Sandwich Factory, naked on the prep table with a dry mouth and pounding headache. The morning shift workers would be arriving any minute.

I dressed and poured myself a Mountain Dew from the soda machine. It was cold and sweet, but my stomach couldn't handle it after a night on Robitussin. I threw up into the prep sink, rinsed away the chunks, then sat down at the manager's desk to write my resignation note.

I affixed it to the cork board with a pushpin and left without locking the door. Fuck Sub-Works. I had too much integrity to spend my life making sandwiches for shitty customers.

I walked to the nearest pay phone and dialled my weed guy. Good news at last, the drought of 1995 was over.

ABOUT THE AUTHOR

J. Archer Avary is a former TV weatherman, champion lionfish hunter, and ferryboat captain. He was born in the USA, became a household name in the Cayman Islands, and now calls the Northeast of England home. His work has been nominated for the Pushcart Prize.

www.avary.co.uk

ACKNOWLEDGEMENTS

Stories in this collection have previously appeared in the following publications:

- BULL
- God's Cruel Joke
- MONO Magazine
- Close to the Bone
- Alien Buddha Press
- Roi Faineant Press
- Many Nice Donkeys
- HASH Journal
- White Wall Review

LEFTOVER
Books